DOG DAY AFTERNOON

ALSO BY DAVID ROSENFELT

DOG DAY AFTERNOON

David Rosenfelt

MINOTAUR BOOKS

NEW YORK

First published in the United States by Minotaur Books, an imprint of St. Martin's Publishing Group

DOG DAY AFTERNOON. Copyright © 2024 by Tara Productions, Inc. All rights reserved. Printed in the United States of America. For information, address St. Martin's Publishing Group, 120 Broadway, New York, NY 10271.

www.minotaurbooks.com

Library of Congress Cataloging-in-Publication Data

Names: Rosenfelt, David, author.
Title: Dog day afternoon / David Rosenfelt.
Description: First edition. | New York : Minotaur Books, 2024. | Series: An Andy Carpenter novel ; 29
Identifiers: LCCN 2024005581 | ISBN 9781250324474 (hardcover) | ISBN 9781250324481 (epub)
Subjects: LCSH: Carpenter, Andy (Fictitious character)—Fiction. | LCGFT: Legal fiction (Literature) | Detective and mystery fiction. | Novels.
Classification: LCC PS3618.O838 D58 2024 | DDC 813/.6— dc23/eng/20240209
LC record available at https://lccn.loc.gov/2024005581

Our books may be purchased in bulk for promotional, educational, or business use. Please contact your local bookseller or the Macmillan Corporate and Premium Sales Department at 1-800-221-7945, extension 5442, or by email at MacmillanSpecialMarkets@macmillan.com.

First Edition: 2024

10 9 8 7 6 5 4 3 2 1

DOG DAY
AFTERNOON

The advertisements are hard to miss.

If you live in North Jersey, in Paterson or quite a few other cities, you are familiar with the phrase **CALL JIM!** It's on billboards, benches, bus stops, and everywhere else that can contain an ad. The all-caps bold type, as well as the exclamation point, unsubtly convey the message that calling Jim is **URGENT!**

The Jim they're referring to is Jim Moore, founder of Moore Law. If you're in an accident, or you slipped and fell on someone else's property, or the surgeon left a sponge in your abdomen, or you sucked down too much asbestos, the ads say that Moore Law is your only way to get financial justice. They will fight and win for you.

If you call and actually want to speak to Jim, you're going to have to yell pretty loud, because one of the things that the ads don't mention is that Jim Moore is dead. He went to that great courtroom in the sky three years ago, but the firm was doing so well that his successors decided not to rock the legal boat by changing the name or the ad campaigns.

The firm has twenty-one offices throughout New Jersey alone. In Passaic County they have three, including one in Paterson, one in Passaic, and one in Clifton. Across the state they employ forty-nine lawyers, seventy-one paralegals, and forty-four admins, with a CEO sitting on top of the entire enterprise.

They are also in ten other states; for a dead guy, Jim Moore has quite an operation going.

If a case is not deemed important, meaning lucrative, there is a good chance that the client meets briefly with a lawyer and then never again gets past the paralegals. But at the end of the day, the people you see and the treatment you get depend on the case you present.

The Paterson office, which is the original Moore Law location and still the main office, is on Market Street in the downtown section. It wasn't a busy day; Fridays in the summer rarely were. The higher-ups often took Fridays off, and most of the other employees left by noon. Everyone could be reached by phone or email if necessary, but pretty much anything other than court appearances could always be put off until Monday.

At four thirty in the Paterson office two lawyers were still present, one of whom was Charles Brisker. Brisker had been with the firm for four years; he came to Moore Law after struggling to maintain his own practice.

Jim Moore had taken a liking to him, and even though Brisker would never be confused with Clarence Darrow, Moore had kept him on. Brisker was not going to be rich or secure a Supreme Court appointment, but he made a comfortable living, and at forty-five was hoping to retire in ten years.

Brisker was meeting with someone in his office, and in addition to the other lawyer, on this Friday afternoon at the Paterson branch of Moore Law four paralegals were in their offices, as well as one admin. None of them were paying much attention to their legal work; they were instead planning what they were going to do on the weekend.

In fact, they were only there that late because they had received an email memo from Brisker requesting that they stay around for a special meeting. It was to take place after his session with the person in his office, and the staff were waiting impatiently for that meeting to end.

None of them heard the noise in the back of the building. There wasn't that much to hear, just the click of a door opening. It would not have attracted any attention even if it was heard; delivery people frequently came in that way. The door remained open, so there was no follow-up thud of it closing.

The man who entered through that door wore a ski mask, incongruous in the summer heat. He was dressed in all black, though his arms were partially bare. On his left arm was a tattoo in the shape of a hook. He moved quickly and with purpose.

He knew where he was going and why.

He had a handgun already out and ready to fire, with another in his pocket in case he needed it, though he knew he would not.

The weapon had a silencer, so when he stopped in Charles Brisker's office, he was able to kill both Brisker and the other man without causing any alarm to the other people in their offices. In each case he fired one bullet directly in the heart; they had barely looked up to see the intruder before they died.

Their killer did not utter a word; he simply moved on. He was just beginning.

Next to die was the admin sitting in the center bullpen. After that, the killer stopped in each paralegal's office. He again used only one bullet for each murder, that was all that was necessary. Each time he said nothing . . . just calmly and methodically gunned the individuals down.

When he reached the other lawyer's office, he found Sally Montrose at her desk. In the adjacent office was a paralegal, Laura Schauble, and the door was open between the two offices.

Montrose looked up at him in terror, seemingly frozen and unable to move as he pointed the weapon at her. "No . . ." was all she could say.

"Sorry, Monty," he said, the first words he had spoken since entering the building. He said it coldly, in a voice that belied the words. He did not sound sorry at all.

He raised the gun, preparing to fire, but then he seemed to hear something from another room, so he quickly lowered the weapon and went to look.

After a few moments, Montrose finally willed herself into action. She locked her door, grabbed her cell phone, and went into the closet, from where she called 911. In a soft voice she told them her location, what was going on, and pleaded for help.

When she hung up, she realized she had not told them who the gunman was. But she did not want to call back and make further sounds. She listened but heard nothing; she was unaware that the others were already dead.

So all she could do was hide until she was rescued.

Six minutes later the police arrived and found Montrose sobbing softly . . . but she was alive and unhurt.

I don't really know or understand Marcus Clark.

That's a strange thing to say about someone that I have worked with for years, and who has literally saved my life on a few occasions. Actually more than a few.

It's not that I don't know things about him. The most obvious of those things is that he is the toughest, scariest person on the planet, and that he combines that physical prowess with an obvious fearlessness.

I have learned that he doesn't have as well-developed a conscience as most people, and that he's an "end justifies the means" guy when it comes to dealing with the criminal element. He believes in justice and makes sure it is administered in whatever way is necessary.

I also know that he's married to Jeannie, a petite blonde who incongruously refers to him as "my little Markie," and that they have a toddler son, Jamie. Jamie must be three years old by now, and based strictly on genetics, he could probably kick my ass already.

I know that Marcus says little, but has no trouble conveying his point of view, and I know he very much likes and respects my wife, Laurie Collins. She's an ex-cop who has earned that respect many times over.

I'm positive that he thinks somewhat less of me, and I'm sure that by now he is well aware I am a physical coward. But he tolerates me, probably because of Laurie.

But I don't really know what makes him tick, and the truth is that I've never made a great effort to learn more. I haven't been that curious, much in the same way that I never tried to figure out where Superman changes into his costume now that phone booths no longer exist.

I've always accepted Marcus on his own terms, since those terms include keeping me alive. His skill at keeping obnoxious defense attorneys breathing is unparalleled, which works for me, since anyone with any knowledge of legal goings-on around here will tell you that I, Andy Carpenter, am as obnoxious as they get.

His ability to keep me alive is particularly timely now, since just yesterday someone walked into a Paterson law office and killed six people. It is probably the worst crime committed in Paterson in my lifetime, and like any urban center, Paterson has seen its share. The killings have left many lawyers uncomfortably looking over their shoulders, me included.

But I learned something new and surprising about Marcus a few weeks ago. He had called Willie Miller, who is my partner in the Tara Foundation. It's a dog rescue operation that we run, named after my golden retriever, who happens to be the best dog in the universe.

I say that with the full knowledge that there might be dogs elsewhere in some distant galaxies. Those alien dogs may be super-advanced, they may travel through time at warp speed and get galactic PhDs, but they would still take a backseat to Tara.

Marcus called Willie to ask if he could bring two young men to the foundation building to see about possibly adopting a dog.

The men were good friends and lived next door to each other, and they would share ownership. When they arrived, they spoke with Willie and he decided they were in fact acceptable for a canine adoption.

Willie is careful about that, and I trust him completely. He's considerably more demanding than I am, and I think I'm fairly strict. Once we rescue a dog, it is under our protection, and we do not take that responsibility lightly.

But the two young men didn't adopt one that day because one of them fell in love with a puppy that has medical issues and isn't yet ready to be adopted. She had been left in front of the local shelter early one morning, with a badly broken leg. She was also quite thin, but she'll be getting excellent, plentiful food from here on out.

We rescued her and our vet set the leg, but it required a metal plate and will take a long time to heal, during which the dog, a golden retriever named Daisy, has to remain relatively inactive. The foundation was the best place to insure that she would get enough rest to heal properly, so the men decided they'd wait for her, which was fine with Willie, and with me.

I haven't seen Daisy yet; she was having a follow-up surgery the last time I was at the foundation. And I wasn't there the day the two guys met her, but I heard all about it.

What surprised me was Willie's description of the connection between the two guys and Marcus. It turns out that Marcus takes troubled young men, often teens but sometimes into their early twenties, and mentors them. He's been doing this for years; apparently he has "graduates" of his program that he keeps in touch with long after they need his help.

Actually, he does more than mentor them. He helps them find a place to live and gets them jobs. Marcus is a fixture in this area

7

and knows a lot of people, few of whom are inclined to say no to him.

When I learned of it, I told Laurie that we should provide financial assistance to Marcus for what obviously is a good cause. We are wealthy due to a significant inheritance I received as well as some lucrative cases I have handled. Marcus makes a good living as an investigator, but surely he could use the help.

Laurie thought it was a good idea and approached Marcus, who shot it down. According to Laurie, he appreciated the offer, but said he could handle things on his own. Laurie's take on it was "Marcus just does not ask for favors."

I thought about that and realized that it was true, at least as it related to me. Marcus has never asked me for anything; he has always done his job and then some, accepted his pay, and moved on.

That is why I am anxious now. Not worried, but anxious. Laurie has just gotten off the phone with Marcus and told me that he's on his way over here to ask for a favor.

"I thought Marcus doesn't ask for favors?"

"He's making an exception. Just this one time."

"Do you have any idea what he wants?"

Laurie nods. "I do."

"What is it?"

"He asked me not to tell you."

"That's fine, but I'm asking you to tell me. I'm your husband, I am claiming the spousal nonsecrecy exception. I can cite you case law on it if you want."

She shakes her head. "Sorry, I promised him. You're going to have to wait; he'll be here in ten minutes, and then you'll know."

"Am I going to like it?"

"No. Definitely not. That much I can say with certainty."

"What should I do when he asks?"

"You should think about how much Marcus has done for you over the years and then make your own decision."

"Uh-oh. Will you support whatever I decide?"

"Of course . . . depending on what you decide."

Laurie was wrong. . . . Marcus is here in eight minutes.
It doesn't seem like much, but even eight minutes can be a long time if you're dreading something. Not that I know why I'm so concerned about this; whatever Marcus asks, I will try to make it happen. He wouldn't ask for something I'm incapable of, so what's the problem?

I doubt that it's money because Laurie said I am not going to like it. I would be happy to give Marcus money; she knows that. And he wouldn't even have to ask me; Laurie and I share our money, so she could have given it to him.

Marcus used to never talk in front of me; he would just grunt and nod. Eventually that changed and Laurie said it was because he got more comfortable with me; I had earned his trust. I have a feeling that in a few minutes I'm going to be longing for the good old grunt-and-nod days.

Marcus, Laurie, and I go into the den. Our thirteen-year-old son, Ricky, has recently gone off on his second summer teen tour with Rein Tours. Last year they went all over the western United States, and this year his group is in France, heading for Spain after that.

The kid has a rough life.

"Marcus, you want me to stay?" Laurie asks.

"Yeah."

We all sit down and I say, "Marcus, how can I help?"

He looks uncomfortable, maybe the first time I've ever seen him this way. "I'm asking you to take a client. I'll pay you."

I have a mixed reaction to this. I've been trying to retire for close to a hundred years, but I can never seem to fully extricate myself from my job. This is going to delay it a little longer, but I'm certainly not going to say no. I'm actually feeling some relief that this is all he's asking.

"Of course. Who is the client?" I'm half expecting Marcus to say it's himself; maybe he's gotten into some kind of trouble.

"Nick Williams."

Marcus said it as if the name is supposed to mean something to me. It doesn't. "Has he been arrested?"

"Not yet. He will be."

"On what charge?" Conversations with Marcus are not easy, even now when he's at his most talkative.

Marcus turns to Laurie, as if for help, and she nods. "Nick Williams has been named as a person of interest in the mass shooting at that law firm," she says. "The police announced it a while ago, while you were walking the dogs."

"They came to me, asking where he was," Marcus says. "He's missing."

"Do you know where he is?"

"No."

"Why did the police come to you?"

"He's a friend."

Laurie explains, "He's one of the young men that Marcus helps."

"Is he one of the guys that came to the foundation to adopt a dog?" I ask, and Marcus nods.

This is turning out to be worse than I expected by a magnitude of about twelve million. "Why do they suspect him?"

"He worked where the shooting took place."

That obviously can't be all. "Do they have evidence connecting him to the shooting?"

Marcus shrugs, and Laurie says, "They must think so, or they wouldn't have gone public."

Time to ask the key question. "Marcus, do you think he could have done this?"

"No."

"Why do you say that?"

"He's good people."

"Do you know any more about it?"

"No."

"Do you know how to find him?"

"No."

"If he contacts you, tell him to turn himself in. A crime of this magnitude, they will find him. If he's armed, he could very possibly not survive the arrest. But the longer that they think he's the killer, the less they will be looking for anyone else."

Marcus nods his understanding.

"There is nothing I can do until he is in custody," I say. "Once that happens, I will do what I can."

"You want some money now?"

"Marcus, what I am about to say is not negotiable. You will not pay me a dime. Whatever I do is because you're my friend."

"I agree with Andy on this," Laurie says. "And we're not budging."

Marcus thinks about it and finally says, "Thanks."

We talk a little more, and I suggest Marcus go home in case Williams shows up there.

When he leaves, Laurie asks, "Have I ever told you that I love you?"

"Not that I recall."

"Well, I do."

"Have I ever told you that I wish I had never gone to law school?"

She smiles. "Yes, I believe you have."

The TV networks that cover the New York metropolitan area are based in New York City.

Since Paterson is only a small part of the region, the news is not exactly "all Paterson, all the time." It takes a major story for Paterson to get any kind of coverage.

The shootings at the Moore Law offices more than qualify. In the three days since it happened, not a newscast goes by without a mention of the progress in the investigation. Or more accurate, the lack of progress.

Actually, the focus quickly moved away from the whodunit; now it's all about finding the guy whodunit. By all accounts, that guy is Nick Williams. But at least for the moment he seems to have effectively disappeared, and the police seem to have no leads as to his whereabouts.

The cops have not come forward with the reasons why Nick is a suspect; they are sitting on whatever evidence they have. But that doesn't matter; just the few known facts are enough for the public to have already voted guilty. That he seems to be on the run cements that view.

Nick Williams worked in that office, didn't show up for work that day, and has now disappeared. He also has two previous arrests, one for assault and one for petty larceny, though neither resulted in convictions. People are also speculating, at least in the media, that he had gang connections. Marcus tells me that the gang rumors are untrue.

His photo has been shown on the news stations repeatedly, and the public has been urged to report any sightings immediately, but not to approach him, as he may be armed and dangerous. Tip lines have been set up but have been fruitless. I have no idea if he will ever be brought to trial, but it's fair to say the jury pool will come tainted.

Laurie and I have been following the story with more than a passing interest, since if Williams is taken into custody, I am going to be knee deep in it.

There's always a chance he won't want me as his lawyer. Maybe he'll see an ad on a bench and decide to "call Jim" to seek representation, though I think the deceased Jim might have a conflict of interest, since they were his employees who were killed. Or maybe one of Williams's alleged previous gang buddies has since gone on and graduated law school.

One lives in hope.

All I can do now is wait and cringe a lot. I also walk the dogs even more frequently than usual, an activity that I always find peaceful.

We have three dogs; the amazing Tara, Hunter the pug, and Sebastian the basset hound. Sebastian makes me look like an exercise fanatic; all he wants to do is sleep and eat. He has long since made his disdain for our walks obvious, so now he uses our backyard as his bathroom. Tara and Hunter are no doubt pleased with this, since it frees them from walking at Sebastian's glacial pace.

I sometimes talk to Tara as we walk. I used to worry that anyone who might be nearby and hear me would think I was nuts, but that's no longer a concern. People walk around conversing through hidden microphones and earpieces all the time, so anyone that sees me can just assume that I'm doing the same.

It used to appear that people talking to themselves were crazy; now they're considered sociable.

"Tara, get used to people looking down on us, or at least down on me. No one likes a lawyer who represents an accused mass murderer, and I'm sorry, but I doubt they'll like his dogs either."

Tara doesn't respond, because even though she is smarter than 90 percent of the people I know, she hasn't mastered the talking thing yet. But I know what she's thinking: I should tell Marcus that I wish I could help, and I'll pay for another lawyer, but this is not something we want to do.

"I can't do that, Tara. This is Marcus we're talking about. He's the only reason I am alive and able to walk with you guys right now."

Tara sort of nods, so I'll take that as her agreeing with me, or at least not arguing the point. I do know that she likes Marcus; he pets her and gives her a biscuit whenever he sees her.

Marcus is a smart guy, and I respect his judgments about people. But that he thinks Nick Williams is innocent of these murders does not impress me. Marcus doesn't have any facts to back up his view, and I would imagine that the prosecution has a boatload of evidence.

And then there is the fact that Williams has apparently fled, which defines consciousness of guilt.

Law enforcement will find him, and if they bring him in alive, he'll be able to tell his story. And then he'll look to his attorney for help.

"Tara, this is looking like a disaster."

That the phone is ringing at 2:35 A.M. is not a good sign.

It jars me awake in the way only a middle-of-the-night phone call, or the sound of one of the dogs vomiting, can do. I look over and see that Laurie is already reaching to answer it. Tara, who sleeps on the bed with us, seems less concerned.

I'm rooting for it to be a wrong number; my second choice is a telemarketer. But I hold out little hope for either, and my pessimism is soon confirmed by Laurie's comment.

After listening for about thirty seconds, she says, "I understand. We'll be there in fifteen minutes." Then she hangs up.

I don't even wait for her to fill me in. "Marcus has him," I say.

She nods and is already starting to get up. "They're in the pavilion at Eastside Park. He called Marcus from a rest stop on the Garden State Parkway. Marcus picked him up and brought him to the park."

"He could have brought him here. Did he say anything about the circumstances?"

"No. But we'll know soon enough."

"You don't need to come."

"I know, but I want to."

We dress quickly and drive to the park, which is less than five minutes away. The pavilion is on the lower level, down where the ball fields are. It once contained a concession stand, but now serves no real function, other than to host meetings between reluctant lawyers and accused mass murderers.

When we arrive, we see that Marcus has not parked on the street, but has instead driven onto the grass near the pavilion. We do the same. It's quite dark out, but there is a decent amount of moonlight, and Laurie has brought a flashlight. I wish she had brought a different lawyer.

Marcus and a young man I obviously assume to be Nick Williams are standing on the steps, waiting for us. Williams is no more than five-nine and is thin, maybe 150 pounds. That wouldn't be any help with a jury; one doesn't have to be particularly strong to pull a trigger.

Before we get a chance to say anything, Williams says, "Marcus told me what happened. I didn't even know about it until Marcus . . . I didn't do it, I swear." Then he repeats, "I swear."

I'm sure Marcus has told him who we are, so I don't bother with introductions. "Where have you been?" I ask.

"I don't know. They took me."

"Who is *they*? And where did they take you?"

"Oh, man," he moans. "I don't know. I just don't know!"

He is clearly agitated, so Laurie says, "Calm down, Nick. I know this is difficult, so just tell us what you do know, as clearly as you can."

Marcus leans in to him and says something, though I can't make out what it is. But Williams nods and takes a deep breath.

"I was leaving for work, going out the back door to the garage. I remember someone grabbed me from behind; I tried to get a look at them, but the next thing I knew I was in a room somewhere. I was chained to a big closed hook sticking out of the wall. I couldn't budge it.

"The room was pretty dark; there was just one lamp and one

window that was blackened out some way. There was a small bathroom and the chain was long enough for me to reach it.

"A few times a day the door opened and two guys were there. They wore masks so I couldn't see their faces, but one was really big; the other was average size. They left me a tray with food each time. I asked them questions, I yelled at them, but they just closed the door and didn't answer me.

"I also yelled for help a lot, but it didn't seem like anyone could hear me. Or at least nobody answered me."

"How long were you there?" I ask.

"I'm not sure. I had no way of knowing if it was day or night, so I lost track. It was probably about three days, but it sure seemed longer."

"How did you get away?" Laurie asks.

"Tonight the same two guys came and got me. They put a mask over my head and put me in the back of a car. I thought they were going to kill me. We drove for quite a while; they took me to a rest stop on the Garden State Parkway, there was no one around because it was the middle of the night.

"They gave me a cell phone; I still have it. They told me to call the cops and turn myself in. I didn't know what the hell that meant . . . or what I would be turning myself in for. I didn't do anything wrong. So as soon as they drove away, I called Marcus. And that's the whole story." Then, "What am I going to do?"

"Do you have an attorney? A criminal attorney?"

"Marcus said you . . . he said you're the best."

"Who represented you at the time of your previous arrests?"

"A public defender."

I nod; this is not going to get any better, so I might as well stop delaying the inevitable. "Okay, the first thing you need to do is exactly what those guys told you. And that is turn yourself in."

"What will happen to me?"

"They'll take you into custody, and then the legal system will take over. But you'll be safe while we deal with this."

"Okay. How do I do it?"

"I'll set it up. Let's go back to our house."

The only positive thing about this entire situation is that I get to wake Pete Stanton up at three thirty in the morning.

Pete is the captain in charge of the Homicide Division of the Paterson Police Department. He's also a close friend, which means we are free to spend our time insulting and annoying each other.

I call him on his cell phone and he answers on the third ring with "Are you okay?" He doesn't sound as if he was sleeping . . . he is alert. Must be a cop thing.

"You're concerned about me. How touching."

"I have now moved past concerned to pissed off. What the hell do you want?"

"I'm about to give you a chance to arrest another innocent person. How many will that be in a row?"

"You have ten seconds to tell me what you want and then I am hanging up. And when I see you, I will strangle you and arrest myself."

"I have Nick Williams with me, and he is offering to turn himself in."

"Where is he?"

"At my house. He's my client."

"This is on the level?"

"It is."

"I'll be right there."

"He is unarmed and is peacefully turning himself in. So tell whatever wannabe Wyatt Earps you bring with you not to do anything stupid."

Click.

Before Pete and his officers arrive I tell Williams not to speak to anyone about anything the entire time he is in custody. I promise to see him at the jail tomorrow, actually today, and we can talk further then.

He seems nervous and more than a little shaken by his ordeal, whatever that ordeal might have been. The Andy Carpenter jury is definitely out on that one.

Pete arrives with six officers, and they professionally take Williams into custody after reading him his rights. The entire thing takes less than five minutes, and they lead him away.

Once they're gone, I realize that Marcus has not said a single word since this began, except for whatever he might have whispered to Williams in the park.

I decide to change that. "Marcus, do you believe him?"

"Yeah," he says, in an outburst of verbiage.

"The whole thing? Including the kidnapping story?"

"Yeah."

"Okay, we'll talk soon and I'll bring the team up-to-date."

He nods and leaves, so I ask Laurie the same question I asked Marcus. "Do you believe him?"

She pauses before answering. "Ordinarily I would say absolutely not. But I trust Marcus's judgment, so I'm keeping an open mind. What about you?"

"I do not. And remember, we're very skeptical and we've only heard his side of the story. We haven't even seen the prosecution's evidence yet."

"You told Marcus you would represent him."

"I vaguely remember that. Which means I am stuck."

Laurie knows that I don't want to take on new clients, and when I do, it will only be in a situation where I believe they are wrongly accused.

"Maybe we'll be surprised," she says.

"Right. Or maybe he'll confess and plead it out."

"Is that what you're rooting for?"

"No. I'm rooting for us, for me, to be wrong about him. Let's get the team together."

"I'll make the calls," she says. "I assume you'll be going down to the jail?"

I nod. "Should be a blast."

The news of the arrest of Nick Williams explodes in the morning media.

On TV they take pains to throw in the word *alleged* every so often, but it's clear that they think the killer has been captured. They even talk about how the people of Paterson can finally breathe easier, free from the danger of violence.

My first call is to Eddie Dowd, the lawyer who assists me when I take on a case. Eddie is a calming influence on me, which is surprising when you consider that in his previous career he was a tight end for the New York Giants.

"We have a client," I say.

"Uh-oh. Is it who I wish it wasn't?"

"It is."

"Can I ask why?"

"Because everyone is entitled to a good defense. And our client says he's innocent."

"Then let's prove it," Eddie says, always the professional. "You want me to ask for discovery?"

"ASAP." We can't do anything until we know what the prosecution has to prompt the arrest. The downside is that we will be revealing to the world that I, Andy Carpenter, am representing Williams. The media will descend on me, and I will be widely reviled.

Business as usual.

Laurie is calling all the members of our team to tell them that we have a client and we'll be meeting as soon as we get more information. In the meantime, I call Sam Willis.

In real life, Sam is my accountant, but in lawyer life, he is what could be referred to as our computer investigator. Sam is a maestro on the keyboard, able to hack into and thereby access literally anything online. Some of it is even legal, but that is usually the least helpful.

He answers the phone on the first ring, as always, with "Talk to me." Then, before I get a chance to "talk to him," he says, "Laurie just called. I'm raring to go."

"Oh, boy. Me too." Sam wants to be a full-time detective, or at least the kind of detective he sees on TV. Certainly he wants shooting to be involved. "Let's get started by learning everything we can about our client's background."

"I'm on it. We looking for a reason he shot up the place?"

"We're on his side, Sam. We're looking to prove he didn't shoot up the place."

"Roger that," Sam says, talking in what he thinks is detective talk. "He's our client so he's innocent, right?"

"Roger that."

Now that I've finished "rogering" with Sam, I head down to the jail to talk to Williams. I still think of him as "Williams," not as my client. At some point that will change, and I might even start thinking of him as "Nick."

But that will take a while . . . it's a process.

I turn on the radio on the way down there and do not yet hear any mention that Williams has hired me as his lawyer. It won't take long; once Eddie has requested the discovery, the news will leak out.

For now I have to announce it to the authorities at the jail. They head off to confirm it, no doubt by asking Williams, so it

David Rosenfelt

takes more than a half hour for me to actually get into the room where I can talk to him.

Two guards usher him in, probably one more than is necessary since he is wearing handcuffs and his legs are shackled. This is a high-profile inmate; they are not taking any chances of a screwup.

I know he has had some experience in the criminal justice system, but this is on a new level, and the fear is obvious in his face. He's accused of being a mass murderer, and that is scary, whether or not he actually is one.

"You okay?" I ask.

He nods. "I guess so. I mean, they're not doing anything bad to me."

"They won't. You haven't talked to anyone, have you?"

"No. There's nobody to talk to anyway. They have me separated from everyone else."

"Good. Let's talk about your situation. Anything you want to add to what you told me last night?"

He shakes his head. "Not really. It's frustrating; I don't know who took me, or why. They didn't ask for money, or try to hurt me, or anything like that."

"You said they knocked you out."

"Right . . . I guess so. I certainly don't remember anything from the time I left my house to the time I woke up in that room."

"Can you think of anyone who has a grudge against you, anything like that?"

"I mean, sure . . . there are guys I knew a few years ago, we didn't all get along. But nothing like this; this wouldn't be their style, you know?"

"Okay, but think about it. What about your friend, the other guy Marcus watches out for?"

"Rafe? My neighbor? He's a good guy; he wouldn't be involved in anything like this."

"His name is Rafe?"

"I think it's short for Rafael. His last name is Duran, but everybody calls him Rafe." Then, "Can I ask you a question?"

"Of course."

"I didn't want to ask anyone here, or the police, but who was . . . who was killed at the office?"

"I don't know all their names, but I'll get them for you. There were six victims; five of them were employees of the firm."

"Damn . . . no matter which people . . . they were my friends."

"You had a good relationship with everyone?"

He nods. "For sure. Definitely. I mean, some better than others, but I didn't have a problem with anybody. And I would never hurt them; I mean, why would I want to?"

I can't answer that. I tell him that I am going to avoid the arraignment and have him file his not-guilty plea with the court. "If that's how you're going to plead," I say.

"Of course. I'm not guilty."

"I understand. But even if you want to change your plea later on, you should plead not guilty now."

"I won't change it. Why no arraignment?"

"Because the press will cover it like the Super Bowl, and the less media attention the better. And while we will still file a motion for bail to be granted, I'm afraid there is absolutely no chance of it. Not for a crime of this dimension and notoriety."

He nods. "Okay, I understand. Whatever you say."

"In the meantime, you need to focus on every moment since you were kidnapped. Try and remember whatever you can about who took you and where you might have been. Anything, no matter how small, could be important."

"I will. Can you find out the names of the people who were killed?"

"Yes. I'll get them to you."

He's quiet for a few moments, then asks, "Why are you helping me? You know I can't pay you much. Is it because of Marcus?"

I nod; no sense in lying to him. "It's because of Marcus."

"Marcus is the best person I've ever met. He's changed my life, and I was no one to him. He never asked for anything in return, just that I be honest with him and be a decent person. He's amazing."

"That he is."

"He also can be a scary guy."

"Really? I hadn't noticed."

I leave the jail and head home; I found it interesting but not particularly revealing that Williams kept asking about the identities of the victims. Obviously if he did the killings, then he's lying about not knowing. So he's either trying to fool me, or he really doesn't know. At this point I don't have a clue which is the case.

I'm in a bad mood already, and it's not going to get any better tonight.

I'm going to an art museum.

The Metropolitan Museum of Art is an enormous building on Fifth Avenue in Manhattan.

It includes over two million square feet of indoor space and draws more than three million visitors every year. The artwork on display is no doubt of mind-boggling value; the Met is firmly entrenched in the major leagues of artland.

I just wish I didn't find it so boring.

I confess that I don't understand much of it; everyone else seems to see something deeper in every piece of art than I do. I like to look at a painting, or a photograph, if it's pretty or interesting, and especially if it tells a story. I look at it and move on, but it seems like all the other people can endlessly stand and stare at it.

The last time I was dragged to a museum, I think it was the Whitney, there was an exhibit by Jasper Johns, a famous and successful artist. He had one piece that was a slice of white bread, literally a slice of actual white bread, on a canvas with a dark background. It was in a frame with a clear glass covering it. I guess that was to prevent it from getting stale, or someone buttering it.

Not surprisingly, the piece was called *Bread.*

People were staring at it, apparently unaware that they could get loaves of the stuff at any 7-Eleven. Plus, they could mix things up; if they wanted, they could switch to rye bread, or whole wheat, whatever they were in the mood for.

I would do better at museums if I could stand on a moving ramp and look at stuff as I go by. A fast-moving ramp. But there are no such ramps at the Met, so I can only go as fast as my legs can carry me.

I'm here as a favor to Robby Divine, who has done me many favors in the past. Robby is the richest person I know, one of the richest that anybody knows, and I've called on his financial expertise, as well as his relationships in that world, for guidance on cases I've worked on.

Robby has organized this charity event, and my role is basically to show up, spend a little time, and write a check. The perk is that I and my fellow attendees get to preview some new exhibits before the public can see them tomorrow.

Goody.

I see Robby in the enormous lobby when I walk in. He's wearing his ever-present Chicago Cubs hat; he's a die-hard Cubs fan who has recently been dying hard as they mostly crash and burn every year.

Robby waves and comes over to me, thanking me for coming. I hand him my check, which he puts in his pocket without glancing at it. We start to walk through the building, entering spacious art-filled room after spacious art-filled room.

"Amazing place, huh?" he asks.

"Yes, it is. You should make an offer on it. If you buy directly from the owner, you won't have to pay a real estate agent."

Robby doesn't respond; for all I know he's considering it. Then he just smiles and goes off to talk with much-richer people than me, leaving me to wander through some rooms full of paintings, understanding little.

In one room I see a woman staring at a painting of what looks to me like a carburetor, but is probably something else. She seems mesmerized by it; maybe she's a mechanic.

There are large printed explanations about each piece and the artist, so I stop to read this one. It says that the artist "takes an avant-garde multidimensional artistic approach that operates at the intersection of abstract expressionism, post-structuralism, and quantum aesthetics."

Got that? This is no ordinary carburetor.

I stand next to the woman, who is still staring at the carburetor.

"Really something, huh?" I say.

She nods, without taking her eyes off the painting. "Extraordinary."

"It seems to operate at the intersection of abstract expressionism, post-structuralism, and quantum aesthetics," I say, showing off.

She still does not look at me; she won't take her eyes off the carburetor. "Obviously."

"One of the most impressive carburetors I've ever seen, and I've been driving all my life."

She doesn't respond, and now she won't get a chance to because a security guard comes over to me. "Mr. Carpenter?"

For a moment I think I'm going to be arrested on a charge of carburetor mocking. But he says, "There is quite a crowd waiting for you outside on the steps; it's causing a bit of a disturbance to our guests."

"Who is it?"

"Mostly the media, but onlookers have gathered to see what is going on. They are waiting for you to come out."

"What are my options here?"

"You can stay and do nothing; you are a guest here. Or we can extricate you through a back exit. Or you can go out and talk to them."

None of the three appeal to me, but I choose door number

three. Obviously, that I am representing Williams is now public; how they found out I was here is a bit of a mystery, but they have their ways, and I might as well get the initial contact over with.

The guard walks me to the door, and I head outside. I stop about ten steps from the bottom, and the media waits for me there. I hold up my hands, as if I am going to conduct a mini–press conference.

"Much as I hate to be drawn away from the incredible artwork, I'll make a statement. Nick Williams is wrongly accused; if it ever gets to trial, which I sincerely doubt, we will prove it in court. He is yet another victim in this horrible tragedy, while the real killer remains at large.

"You can follow me around all you want, but I won't be speaking publicly about this case again until the charges are dropped, or a jury says 'not guilty.' Thanks for coming."

With that I walk down the rest of the steps, and they part to let me go through. They follow me to the parking lot, yelling questions, but I don't acknowledge them. Hopefully at some point they'll give up.

It's been a really fun day.

I f there is one aspect of a case that I hate the most, and there are many contenders for that honor, it would be the initial reading of the discovery material.

It tells us everything about the law enforcement investigation to date, and since it has resulted in the arrest of our client, it is by definition one-sided and terrible.

The prosecution is obligated to include in the discovery anything they have come up with that is exculpatory to the defense. Good luck finding anything.

Eddie Dowd has brought the initial discovery documents to the house this morning and has had to navigate the media horde that is stationed in the street outside. Actually, there are less of them than I expected; maybe they took my vow not to comment further seriously.

Eddie declines Laurie's offer of something to eat, instead opting for coffee. Once his cup is filled, we head into the den to learn the bad news.

"Have you looked through it yet?" I ask.

"No. I thought you'd want to share that honor. By the way, I found out who the prosecutor is that is handling the case."

"Who?"

"Richard Wallace."

"Richard? He's doing it himself?"

"Yes."

I'm not happy to hear this. Richard is head of the department, so it's no surprise that he would assign himself. It's basically a no-win proposition for a prosecutor: If he gets a conviction, then he's just doing what everyone expects him to do. If he somehow loses, then the criticism will be deafening, and possibly job and career threatening.

Richard would hesitate to put that burden on anyone else, so he's putting himself on the line. I would expect nothing less. It's safe to say that Richard Wallace is my only friend in the prosecutor's office and the only one there who doesn't despise me.

Our connection is through my father, the late Nelson Carpenter, who had the top prosecution job before Richard did. My father was a mentor to Richard, who was therefore close to our family. So I got to know him more as a friend and almost a sibling than an opposing counsel.

I not only like him, but I respect him and his ability, which is why I wish he weren't on this case. He's probably the least likely in the department to make a key mistake, and by far the least likely to be unnerved by my unconventional and annoying style.

"Which judge has been assigned?" I ask.

"Ramirez."

I'm okay with that. A total of zero judges in North Jersey like me and my style in court, but Nestor Ramirez tolerates me more than most.

There is a lot of discovery for this stage of a case, which reflects the intensity of the investigation, which in turn reflects the seriousness of the crime. As we go through the files, we see that a huge part of it is the forensics. There is by unfortunate definition a lot of blood evidence at a mass murder scene.

It takes Eddie and me three hours to look through it all, and

I don't think we say ten words to each other the entire time. It's important that we digest everything; it's an excellent feature of the justice system that the defense learns what the opposition is relying on.

It would be akin to my Giants being gifted the Dallas Cowboys' playbook well before the game. We'd probably still lose, but we wouldn't be surprised in the process.

So far there is not a great deal of evidence against Williams, but what is here is devastating. It mostly centers on two witnesses, the main one a lawyer named Sally Montrose. She works in the Moore Law office where the murders took place, and she was one of two survivors of the shooting.

She says that she was about to be shot herself, but as the killer was preparing to fire, he was somehow distracted. She reports that the killer called her Monty, a nickname used by everyone in the office, including Nick Williams. She also says that she recognized his voice, though in the interview she doesn't seem quite as certain of that as of the rest of the things she relates.

Most significant, she also saw a tattoo of a hook on the killer's left arm, which is distinctive and matches that on Williams's left arm, and she recognized his sneakers, which have red and yellow stripes on them.

As related in the transcript, the police officer asked if she was positive it was Nick. "As sure as I can be," she said. "There was the tattoo, the sneakers, and the way his voice sounded when he called me Monty. He also walked the way Nick walked. It was definitely him; I knew it before he said a word."

There is also another witness, Laura Schauble, a paralegal who was with the firm for six years. She was hiding in the office adjacent to Montrose's and heard the killer through the open door. She escaped, and Montrose thinks that the noise Schauble made in doing so might have caused the killer to be distracted and concerned, thereby saving Montrose's life. Schauble also heard the use of the nickname Monty.

Her comments in the interview are not quite as damaging as Montrose's, but they're not good: "I didn't see his face from where I was. But there was this open area on his arm between his glove and sleeve. So I saw the tattoo. But I didn't see his other arm, so I don't know if there was a second gun."

"Did you hear him speak?"

"Yes. He said, 'I'm sorry, Monty.'"

"Did you recognize his voice?"

"I don't know for sure, but it definitely sounded like it could have been Nick."

The rest of the incriminating evidence is circumstantial, which does not equate to insignificant. Most important is that Williams took off from work that day without notifying anyone, which was uncharacteristic. And then there is the fact that he disappeared for days after the shooting, despite that the entire world was looking for him and announcing it in the media.

There is no mention of motive, at least not yet. The prosecution doesn't have to demonstrate motive, but they always want to. In this case it can be only one of two things: either Williams was a disgruntled, bitter employee, or he is nuts. "Nuts" opens the door to an insanity defense, so I am sure they will ultimately go with "disgruntled."

One thing is for sure: despite the tremendous pressure to quickly solve the case, there was no rush to judgment here. The evidence they had was more than enough to justify the arrest.

Of course I will claim a rush to judgment; to do otherwise would be to violate the defense attorney's credo. If the prosecution pondered the evidence for a decade, I would still find a way to claim that they had rushed to judgment.

Nowhere in these documents does the prosecution assert that they know where Williams was during the time between the shootings and his arrest. If they subsequently figure that out, and it disproves his contention that he was kidnapped, it would be game, set, and match.

And my client would never see the light of day again.

Thank here are crime scenes, and then there are crime scenes. The one at the Moore Law offices is one I am not going to forget anytime soon.

Laurie and I always visit the crime scene together on any case I am working on. It's not a husband-and-wife togetherness thing, though I certainly recommend it to couples who want to spice up their relationship. I bring her because, as an ex-cop, she can often see things that I can't.

At least half a dozen current cops are guarding the place, mostly to keep sightseers out. I'm sure members of the Paterson Ghouls Club would love to rummage around in here. Eddie Dowd spoke to Richard Wallace, and Richard cleared our entry; when we walk in, I'm sorry he did.

Little has been cleaned up, and our being told to put these rubber booties on our shoes is evidence that the forensics people must think more work could be done. They didn't have to worry about me; I'm not going to be stomping around in blood.

We walk from room to room; it's easy to tell where each of the murders was committed just from the bloodstains. One took place in the center area, three in small individual offices, and two in the larger office. There's actually less blood than I expected, but it's still horrifying.

We also go into the back to see where the killer apparently

entered. The door is closed, so we open it and look into the back alley. The killer most likely escaped the same way he came in.

The cold-blooded nature of the shootings is obvious and chilling. This was not someone who came in with an assault rifle and started shooting indiscriminately. This was someone who hunted down his victims and killed them, one after another.

"I think this was done by a professional," Laurie says.

"Why?"

"He was totally methodical. He went from room to room, like he was checking off boxes. He was obviously an excellent shot. And there was no anger here; if there was, he would have used more than one bullet on each person."

"I agree. But this was not a random shooting; the killer knew the layout and knew where he was going. He also knew the nickname of one of the survivors. That implicates Williams."

"You said the witness reported he was wearing a hood concealing his face?"

"Yes."

"Also rare in a mass shooting, and another sign of lack of anger. In most cases the killer is not worried about getting caught in the moment; he often expects to die himself. Suicide is common."

I nod. "And if everyone is going to be killed, who was he concealing his identity from?"

"Were there video cameras in the office?"

"No, and not in the back alley either."

"Too bad. Does the discovery speculate as to what might have distracted the killer and prevented him from shooting the last woman?"

"*Speculate* is the right word. Come down here." We walk down to Sally Montrose's office; I know it from the layouts of the office in the discovery. Once we get there, I say, "Sally Montrose was sitting there, at her desk. Another paralegal, Laura Schauble, was next door, and that door between the two was open.

"Schauble heard what was happening and escaped. Montrose believes the killer heard her leave and went to find her. He didn't succeed, and they further speculate that he panicked that the police would come soon, so he didn't return to finish Montrose off."

"Doesn't seem consistent with how he handled everything else. This does not seem like the type of person to deviate from his plan, or to panic."

"Right," I say. "He was completely methodical, but for some reason he didn't return to kill Montrose. Maybe he wanted a witness."

Laura does a mini–double take. "Are you starting to believe Williams is telling the truth?"

"I'm a long way from saying that. But I would like to know what would make a guy like that walk in and coldly gun down six people, five of whom he worked with."

"Somebody did."

"No question about that. And whoever did it had a reason. If we can find out the reason, we find the killer."

've been through this too many times to be sure this is going to trial.

A lot can and often does happen before then. Most often the accused, faced with overwhelming, irrefutable evidence, decides it's in his best interest to plead it out. Far less frequently, exculpatory evidence comes to light that causes the prosecution to drop the charges.

But if the Nick Williams case does go to trial, it will require an intense amount of effort and dominate my life. So I'm going to devote the rest of this day to normalcy; tomorrow the team meets to get started, and normalcy will be in the rearview mirror.

My first stop is the Tara Foundation. I try to get here as often as I can, though Willie Miller and his wife, Sondra, do all the real work. But once the case begins, my visits here will be rare, so I want to at least check in.

I tell Willie that I have a client, so I apologize in advance for my future absences. As always, he and Sondra are fine with it and tell me I have nothing to feel guilty about.

"A murder case?" he asks.

I nod. "Yeah. The mass shooting down at that law office."

"No kidding? You're representing the guy who did it?"

"No, I'm representing the guy they're accusing. His name is Nick Williams."

"I heard about that," Willie says. "I recognized the name

because Marcus brought around a guy named Nick Williams. Good kid."

"That's the client."

"Come on," Willie says, clearly disbelieving. "No way."

"I kid you not. You didn't see his picture on TV?"

"We don't watch much TV. I watch sports and Sondra does that streaming stuff. She's going to be upset about this."

"Why?"

"Come on, I'll show you."

He takes me into the office, where a special large dog cage has been set up. In it is Daisy, the golden retriever puppy, with a cast on her leg. Daisy had been left in front of the local shelter, probably by an asshole owner who had no interest in treating her leg.

The shelter called us because there was no way they would have the resources or inclination to fix her badly broken leg. If we didn't take her, they would have put her down. Putting down a golden retriever defines *unacceptable.*

So we rescued her and had paid for a complicated surgery, which involved putting a plate in the leg. There was then a follow-up surgery. She will eventually be fine, but she has to be confined for almost twelve weeks, to give the leg a chance to heal.

Daisy is beautiful, which is redundant when talking about golden retrievers. She has a great smile and a tail that at the moment is wagging at full speed, banging at the side of the cage that confines her. It's been a rough start to her life, but we will make sure it gets a lot better.

"Daisy is the dog Nick Williams fell in love with," Willie says.

"Okay." I already knew that, and I'm not sure where Willie is going with this.

"He came here every night, after work, for two weeks, to sit with Daisy and pet her in the cage. Every night. Last week he stopped coming, and now I know why."

I'm impressed, but not convinced this has any great meaning other than that Nick likes dogs, Daisy in particular. "What's your point, Willie? You think he couldn't have done the shooting because he came to pet Daisy?"

"No, I think he couldn't have done the shooting because I talked to him a lot when he was here. He's a great kid. Sondra will feel the same way."

I nod. "I'll do my best to get him and Daisy back together."

Willie smiles. "You'll get it done."

I met Willie when I won his appeal after he was wrongly convicted of murder, so he has a tendency to overrate my legal talents.

From the foundation I head down to Charlie's, the best sports bar / restaurant east of the Pacific Ocean. I assume it's also the best one west of the Pacific as well, but I haven't done enough due diligence on the matter.

I used to go to Charlie's at least five nights a week; I still share a reserved table with Pete Stanton and Vince Sanders, who is editor of the local newspaper. They are probably my two closest nonfamily friends, which means we can insult each other, expose each other's deepest vulnerabilities, commit relentless emotional torture, and nobody takes offense.

If Vince and Pete do resent it, they are likely not to show it because I pay for all the food and drink that they consume at Charlie's, whether I am there or not. I'm not sure how that came about, but they are certainly not going to give up the perk now that they have it. The result is that my tab number increases like a telethon tote board. If that embarrasses them, they conceal it well.

I don't bother calling either of them to find out if they will be there, since the only way they wouldn't is if they were dead, in which case they wouldn't answer the phone.

Sure enough, when I arrive, they are already here, drinking beer, stuffing their faces with burgers and french fries, and watching the Mets game on one of the many televisions that dot the place. My empty chair awaits me, and as I smoothly slide into it, I say, "What a surprise finding you two losers here."

"Be careful, or we'll start drinking champagne," Vince says.

"I doubt that. You're barely sophisticated enough to drink beer."

"You came here to insult us?" Pete asks.

"Pretty much."

The waiter, Chris, springs into action when I sit down. Since I always have a burger with no cheese, french fries so burnt that their french fry friends and relatives would need dental records to identify them, and a Diet Coke, he doesn't wait for me to order.

In addition to having a relaxing night, I have another reason for coming here tonight. As the head of Paterson PD Homicide, and the arresting officer in the Nick Williams case, Pete obviously has special insights into the prosecution's case.

I always try to coax some information tidbits out of him. I rarely succeed, but one lives in hope.

Between innings, he brings it up. "How's your case going, counselor? You plead it out yet?"

"No chance."

"Good," Vince says. "It's a better story if you lose at trial. I've got three reporters assigned to watching you crash and burn."

"Thanks, Vince. But it won't happen; I mean, what are the odds that Pete arrested the right guy? You've got more chance of getting a date."

"Right," Pete says. "Williams didn't do it and then happened to leave town; he spent the three days after the shooting at a religious retreat."

"You have any evidence about where he was?"

"We will." Pete smiles smugly. "But maybe you can explain it?"

I return the smug smile, secretly glad to hear that they don't know where Williams was. "There are explanations for everything."

"Wow," Vince says. "That's profound."

"What's the explanation for his knowing the witness's nickname at work?" Pete asks.

"He isn't the only one who knew it; everybody did. Just like everyone refers to you as 'asshole.'"

"How'd you like me to drown you in your Diet Coke?" Pete asks.

"Now, now," Vince says. "Take it easy, Pete. We don't want to start getting a check when we finish here, do we?"

"Andy's tab is the only thing keeping him alive," Pete says.

Vince turns to me. "You hear that? You better keep paying; I don't want anything bad to happen to you."

"Your concern is touching, Vince."

"It's called being a good friend."

Having a team meeting to start a case feels like the legal equivalent of beginning a trek up Mount Everest.

This is the beginning of what will be an intense process under constant pressure. Our client's life is on the line, and we literally represent his only defense.

They say that in a trial the prosecution has the burden, in that they must prove the case beyond a reasonable doubt. The defense doesn't have to prove anything. But it's the defense that has the emotional burden. If we lose, Williams spends the rest of his life behind bars. If the prosecution loses, they go home to their families and get to work on their next case.

The team is assembled in the conference room in my office. By any standard, the place is a dump, occupying most of the second floor above Sofia Hernandez's fruit stand on the street level.

Sofia is also my landlady; she's a terrific person who somehow gets summer fruit nine months of the year. If the big law firms knew that, they'd be fighting to get in this building.

When Laurie and I arrived, everyone else was already assembled. It's not easy to all fit into this room, and if the air conditioner wasn't working, I doubt we'd live for more than an hour.

Present are Marcus Clark, Eddie Dowd, Sam Willis, and Corey Douglas, an ex-cop who is part of an investigative team with Laurie and Marcus. Also here are Willie Miller, who told me that he wants to help Nick Williams, and Edna, my office manager.

I'm surprised to see Edna, and not only because she avoids actual work at all costs. Edna got engaged a couple of years ago to a wealthy, retired businessman, and they have spent most of that time traveling the world to find the perfect place for their destination wedding. The last I heard they were in the strangely named Bora Bora; I've never quite understood why one *Bora* wasn't sufficient.

I can picture its founding fathers getting together to name their country. Since *Tahiti* was taken, one of them suggested *Bora,* but the others didn't think that was strong enough. They doubled the *Bora*s, and a nation was born.

In any event, I had offered Edna and her fiancé my office for the wedding ceremony, but they declined.

Before I take my seat, Edna asks if she can talk to me in another room. I can't imagine what this is about, but I'm dreading it. Maybe she's going to retire, although in terms of actual work done, she retired a decade ago. She's just continued getting and cashing checks.

"What's going on, Edna?" I ask, when we are in my office and out of earshot of the others. "How's the destination hunting going?"

"This is going to come as a shock. But David and I have decided to go our separate ways."

"Oh. I'm sorry to hear that. I didn't realize . . ." I stop talking because I have no idea how to finish the sentence; I'm not even sure why I started it. Please, someone, get me out of this office.

"We could not decide on a destination. I wanted Paris, and he wanted Bangkok. Do I want to be with someone who picked Bangkok as a place to be married?"

"Apparently not."

"There were other reasons, but I'm not sure I should share them."

DON'T SHARE THEM! is what I scream in my mind, but my mouth says, "Some things are better kept private."

She nods. "Anyway, if I'm not as intensely into my work as usual, I hope you'll understand."

"I totally will, Edna. We'd better get back into the conference room; the trial is coming up."

We go back in and I get things started. "So, as you know, we have a client, Nick Williams. And as you definitely know, he's accused of the mass shooting at the Moore Law offices last week in which six people lost their lives.

"Marcus knows Nick very well, and Willie also has a relationship with him. They both vouch for his good character, but unfortunately they will not be on the jury. Sam, what have you learned about him so far?"

Sam stands, holding some papers but not looking at them as he speaks. "I don't have much yet, but will look deeper if we need me to. Williams was left an orphan at six years old; it's not clear whether his parents abandoned him or were deceased.

"He wound up in three different foster homes . . . not sure why he was moved around so much. He had a few juvenile arrests, but the details are under seal. I can penetrate it if you decide it's necessary."

"No need to do that, Sam," I say.

"Williams is twenty-two years old and has had two arrests as an adult, one for a street fight outside a nightclub eight months ago, and another for a convenience store petty theft. The charges were ultimately dropped in both cases.

"He has worked at Moore Law as a combination handyman and delivery person for seven months, until the events of the other day."

Sam sits down, so I say, "Thanks, Sam. The bottom line is that someone walked into that office and killed those people. Our position, of course, is that it was not our client, so we are going to have to find out who did. And the key way to do that is to find out why they did it."

"Does Williams have an alibi?" Corey asks.

"He says that he was kidnapped by persons unknown that morning, kept in a room for three days, and then released. He does not know who took him or where they kept him, and while he was in captivity, he was unaware of the events at the law office."

Corey frowns slightly; as he's an ex-cop, I'm sure he doubts Williams's story. Jurors will have the same reaction if and when they hear it.

"Let's go at this two ways," I say. "We need to look into who might have had a grudge against the firm or any of the victims. Sam, you should start by doing a background check on those victims.

"Then we'll want to try and prove our client's story. If we can confirm it, we'll have a major leg up. And if we can find out who kidnapped him, we'll also have our killers.

"Laurie will give out the assignments. Marcus, as the person closest to Williams, do you have anything to say?"

Marcus, who absolutely never talks in meetings, nods slightly and stands up. "Nick is good people," he says, so softly it's hard to hear him. "He didn't do it." Then he sits down.

For Marcus that compares to Hamlet's soliloquy, and the room is quiet as it sinks in.

"You heard the man," I say. "Let's prove it."

Usually when I need to meet with Richard Wallace about a case, we have lunch or dinner in a restaurant.

Richard and I are friends . . . have been so for many years . . . so we use the meetings as a time to catch up on each other's life. As I mentioned, my father was like a father to Richard, which would make us brothers.

I don't see him as often as either of us would like, but when we do, we immediately pick up where we left off.

This time our meeting place is different: Richard called to suggest we meet in his office. It's not that the case will come between us; we've been through enough legal battles to know that won't happen. It's more that the media could get wind of our meeting, disrupt us with questions, and endlessly speculate about it.

I arrive at the prosecution offices and walk down the long hallway to Richard's office, which used to be my father's. There are a lot of memories for me here; as a kid I used to visit my father here often.

This time is very different. Along the way I pass Richard's colleagues, all of whom despise me. Their stares of hatred give me a warm feeling.

Once I'm in Richard's office, he greets me with a big smile

and a small hug. We sit and chat for a while, drinking Diet Cokes. He asks about Laurie and Ricky, and I send my regards to his wife, Sharon. I know where this is going, but I'm in no hurry to get there. I would imagine he feels the same way.

Finally he says, "So where do we stand?"

"I'm not sure yet. I'm really just getting into it. But it looks like you have the wrong man."

He smiles. "Come on, Andy."

I return the smile. "So I haven't convinced you? What about if I say it with more charm and apparent sincerity?"

"I don't think even that will do it. In addition to everything else, he ran, and it wasn't because he was afraid the cops were blaming him. He disappeared even before his name came out."

"There are explanations for everything."

"I'd love to hear this one."

"I don't think I'm quite ready to share it. But you could do me a favor."

"What's that?"

"Try and use your influence to get the cops to keep looking into this." I say this even though there is no chance it will have any impact.

"The investigation is definitely ongoing, Andy."

"Yeah, they're trying to find more evidence against Williams. I'd rather they used some resources to find the real killer."

"Pete has an open mind," Richard says, referring to Pete Stanton.

I shake my head. "Pete's an outstanding cop; please do not tell him I said that. But he's still a cop. And when cops think they have the right man, they stop looking for anyone else."

Richard nods. "I hear you. I'll speak to him. But it looks bad for you, Andy."

I decide to change the subject. "What do you think of Steven Loomis? I assume you know him?" Loomis is the CEO of Moore Law. He works out of the Paterson office, but was not in the day of the shooting.

I have a call in to Loomis to request a meeting, but haven't heard back yet. I imagine he has quite a bit on his plate right now, so it's understandable.

Wallace shrugs. "I know him. He's a bit of an empty suit, but that business is a big success. It feels like he just was in the right place at the right time to end up as the head of it, but maybe that's not giving him enough credit.

"Jim Moore never dreamed of making the money they're making now, but I don't think they've structured themselves to handle it well. They still run it like a mom-and-pop store, at least that's what I've heard."

"Sounds like mom and pop are raking it in. So why am I here? Do you have an offer to make that I can turn down?" Usually these meetings result in the prosecution offering a reduced but significant sentence in return for a guilty plea.

"Actually, no. It's too high profile, and too awful an offense. Of course we would welcome a guilty plea to avoid the expense of a trial, but no reduced sentence will be offered. I do have a question, though. Why did you take the case?"

Richard knows that I want to work as little as possible, and only when I think the client is innocent. He doesn't believe I could think that of Williams.

"Marcus. Marcus swears by him. That carries a lot of weight with me."

Richard nods. "Interesting. Anyway, I'm glad we had a chance to catch up."

"So am I. And you know I love coming down here. I have so many close friends among your colleagues."

He laughs. "Did they throw rose petals at you as you walked down the hall?"

"Actually, I think they were knives."

The next crime scene Laurie and I are visiting is unusual.

That's because in this case we are hoping it's actually a crime scene; our case and our client's chances for an acquittal probably depend on its being one.

We're at the garden-apartment complex in Clifton where Nick Williams lives, or at least where he lived before moving into the Passaic County jail. He had a studio apartment next door to Rafael "Rafe" Duran, the other young man who Marcus has been mentoring.

Duran is not home now; he's at work. That's fine; we'll come back and talk to him later. Right now we just want to see the place and judge the credibility of Williams's story, since the jury may be judging it themselves at trial. Of course, there's no guarantee that the jury will even hear it. We're a long way from that.

Corey Douglas has been canvassing the neighborhood, talking to the residents, and he told Laurie that he'll meet us here, because he has someone he wants us to talk to. But for now we're just checking out the place, especially the area behind the house, where Williams says the kidnapping took place.

The eight identical units have four apartments each, separated on each side from its neighbor by a driveway. A common garage sits in the back at the end of each of those driveways.

Laurie and I walk the length of the one adjacent to Williams's unit, on the right. At the end is the garage where he kept his car. Laurie goes directly to it and lifts the door open. She doesn't bother putting on gloves or being careful since the presence of powder indicates that the cops have already dusted the handle for prints.

"No automatic opener necessary," she says. "Anyone could have gotten in."

We look into the garage and see only one car, a fairly beaten-up Chevy Malibu.

"Is that Nick's?" She's started to use Nick's first name; I still refer to him as Williams.

"Yes. It matches what he told me." I point to the back door of the apartment unit. "He says he left through that door, as he always did, and at some point between there and the garage they grabbed him. That's all he remembers."

"They knocked him out?"

"He doesn't know, but he had no bruises, so maybe they used some kind of drug, or anesthesia."

"And they had a car?"

I shrug. "He and I have no idea."

"But they must have driven here and taken him off in their car."

"Right. This is going to be hard for a jury to buy into."

Laurie doesn't answer for a while, a sure sign that she agrees with me. Then, "So three days later they dropped him off at the rest stop."

I nod. "Which is what he says happened." Then, "But there is one thing which might corroborate his story."

"What's that?"

"If he had no car, and if they didn't drop him off at the rest stop like he claims, then how did he get there? And if he somehow did have his car, and Marcus picked him up at the rest stop, then how did the car get back here?"

"Good point."

We're interrupted by Corey walking up the driveway with a man who I would estimate is in his late twenties. He must be the neighbor that Corey said we should speak with.

Corey introduces him as George Truesdale, and George tells me that he's seen me on television and that it's "really cool" to meet me. Obviously George is a quality individual.

"Tell them what you told me," Corey says.

George nods. "Okay, sure. Am I going to have to testify or anything?"

"We're a long way from that, George. Let's hear what you have to say first."

"Okay. Nick is a buddy of mine; we hang out a lot. I work near the law office where he did. I'm a cashier at the 7-Eleven on Market Street." Then, probably feeling the need to explain, he adds, "Today's my day off."

"Okay," I say, because the conversation seems to be lagging.

"So Nick would give me a ride to work and back. I live a couple of blocks that way; he'd pick me up. But on that day, he didn't show."

"Which day?"

"You know . . . the day those people got killed."

"Had Nick been acting in any way unusual the last time you saw him?"

"No, but I hadn't seen him in a few days. The day before, he got his car serviced, so he didn't drive me then either."

I make a mental note to check into the car servicing, then ask, "So what did you do when he didn't show up that day?"

"I called him to see what was going on, but he didn't answer, so I walked down here. As I got near the house, a car was pulling out of the driveway. There was a guy driving; looked like a big guy but it was hard to tell. And there was another guy in the backseat."

"You didn't know who they were?" Laurie asks.

"No, but it seemed weird. I mean, the passenger seat in the front was empty, but the other guy was in the back. Like it was a cab or something, but it was a regular car."

"What kind of car was it?" I ask.

"I don't know. Just a regular car . . . black or dark blue. I'm not really into cars. But I never saw it before, and I never saw them before, and Nick wasn't around. It wasn't like Nick. Then when the shooting happened, and they were looking for Nick, I thought it might mean something."

"Would you recognize those guys in the car again?"

"Sorry, but I don't think so."

"George, if you think of anything else, anything at all, call Corey, okay?"

"Sure, but I told you everything. Will this help Nick?"

"It might, George. It just might."

Our conversation with George Truesdale has had a major effect on my attitude toward this case: I too am now thinking of my client as "Nick."

Actually, that's a secondary effect. The real change is that Truesdale's story fits in so well with what Nick has told me that I have an increased glimmer of hope that Nick might be telling the truth.

Of course, not every "hope glimmer" turns out to be meaningful; for example, at one point last year I hope-glimmered that the Mets could get to the World Series. And I hope-glimmered a date with Nancy Dolman my entire senior year in high school. It turned out that Nancy had the exact opposite hope glimmer and hers prevailed.

Hope glimmering is a zero-sum game.

The two people that Truesdale saw might have had nothing to do with Nick; eight apartments are adjacent to that driveway. And that the passenger sat in the back might well be of no significance; for all I know the car was an Uber.

But it tends to at least be consistent with Nick's story, and even though Truesdale's recounting of events would carry little weight in court, it tends to make this lawyer feel better.

I am also starting to think in terms of trial strategy. Nick's story could at this point only be told by Nick; no one else could testify to it. Like all defense attorneys, I would only put my client on the stand as a last resort; there's too much chance of a cross-examination disaster.

Besides, Nick's story has huge holes, even as he tells it. Where was he for three days? He doesn't know. Why was he taken? He doesn't know. Who took him? He doesn't know.

The position of the defense, at this point, is that he was taken to set him up for the shootings. The tattoo, plus the referring to the witness by her nickname before keeping her alive to testify, was a setup to make things point even more clearly to Nick.

Our theory, such as it is, makes sense, as long as one believes the kidnapping narrative. Getting the jury to believe it is going to be a neat trick.

The use of the nickname Monty for Sally Montrose is particularly interesting. It shows that the real killer was familiar with her, whether through work or somewhere else. The methodical way he went through the office, apparently knowing exactly where he was going, also shows that it was an inside job.

Unfortunately the prosecution completely agrees with our assessment and uses it to point to Nick. He knew Montrose and he knew the office layout.

Laurie and I order a pizza in for dinner. Her suggesting it is a rare treat and surprise. Usually I use Ricky to try to arrange a pizza dinner; I get him to beg for it. It's not something I'm proud of. But with him away on the teen tour, I have so far suffered through a pizza-less summer, so I grab at this opportunity.

I bring up the mass murder case over dinner because I am at heart an incurable romantic. "We have two areas of possible motive. One is that the killer was striking back at the law firm for reasons unknown."

"And two?"

"That one of the people killed was the target, and the rest were collateral damage. It was an effort to cover up that there was one intended victim; this way that victim would get lost in the crowd."

"I'm picking door number one . . . some issue at the firm," Laurie says. "The killer knew Nick; they knew where he lived, they knew about his tattoo, and they probably knew something of his checkered background. And the use of the nickname shows a connection to the firm as well."

I think she's right, but at the moment my mouth is too full of pizza to verbalize it. My technique is to eat all the cheese-covered areas of the pie, then nibble on the crusts afterward. And if I'm full, or even if I'm not, I can give pieces of the crust to Tara, Hunter, and Sebastian.

Laurie never eats her crust, so the dogs love it when we get pizza.

"But I think we should look at both possibilities," she says, echoing something I would have said when I finished chewing. Pizza tends to put me at a conversational disadvantage.

"I will look at the possibilities that it was revenge against the firm," I say. "You, Marcus, and Corey should do a deep dive on each of the deceased. Sam already has information to give you a head start."

Once we're done, I call Sam and ask him to update everyone on whatever information he has gotten on the victims.

"Will do," he says. "You think one person was the target?"

"It's one of a number of working theories."

"That's pretty cold."

He's right; if the killings were indeed done to target only one person, then it shows a horrifying disregard for human life. Of course, in a mass murder that horrifying, disregard is there whatever the motive.

"You need anything else?" Sam asks.

"Yes. I want to know as much as I can about the firm. How they're set up, how they make their money, if they have had any well-publicized disputes lately . . . and I don't mean just legal."

"I'm on it. When do you need it?"

"Yesterday."

"Figures. Anything else?"

"Funny you should ask. Nick left his house at around seven thirty in the morning the day of the shooting. I want to know if any cell phones belonging to nonresidents were there."

Sam has the less than legal ability to cyber-enter phone company computers and access the GPS records that all cell phones generate. Sam prefers the phrase *cyber-enter* to *hack*; he considers it more dignified.

"A lot of people live there," he points out, accurately. "There will be a lot of phones to cull through, with different providers, and I don't have a list of residents."

"Sounds like an easy problem for you to overcome."

"Yeah, right. There also might be guests, possibly delivery people. How will I know who to look for?"

"Concentrate on nonresident phones that arrived in the area not very long before seven thirty and left shortly thereafter. And I doubt they have returned."

"Okay. Do I have more time on this one?"

"I'm thinking no."

"Can I go now? I have a lot of work to do."

"Of course. I'm an agreeable guy."

Sam hangs up and I am about to take the dogs on a long walk when Eddie Dowd calls.

"I've got some bad news," he says.

"That is probably my least favorite sentence. What is it?"

"They found the murder weapon in a dumpster a block away from Nick's house. It took until now to do the forensics on it."

"Let me guess. This is about to get worse."

"It is. They got Nick's print off it."

According to Marcus, Rafe Duran is Nick Williams's best friend.

I haven't confirmed that with Nick, and I will, but right now it is pretty low on my list of priorities. For example, it ranks below my trying to explain away how Nick's fingerprint is on the murder weapon.

Duran is the other young man currently under the protective wing of Marcus Clark. He lives in the unit next door to Nick's and works as a detailer at a car wash in downtown Paterson. Marcus apparently got him the job, as he got Nick his job at the law firm.

Duran asked me if I could meet him during his break. Since the car wash is just a few blocks from my house, it was convenient for me to do so. We meet at a coffee shop next door, and I get there just before he does.

He recognizes me; maybe he's seen me on television. Being a big-time celebrity lawyer has its advantages.

"How is Nick?" he asks, as we are on the way to our table.

"He's hanging in there."

We reach the table and sit down. "Can I visit him?"

"Yes. I'll get your name on the list. But when you're there, don't ask him to talk about the case." Conversations between prisoners and their guests are, shall we say, prone to being overheard.

"Is he going to beat this?"

"How long do we have to talk?"

"My boss said I needed to be back in a half hour."

"Then order some food if you want it, but let me ask the questions, okay?"

I call the waiter over and he orders a burger and fries; we obviously share the same taste in food. I just get a Diet Coke.

"How long have you known Nick?"

"About two years. We met at a pickup basketball game in Nash Park, and we became buddies."

"Are you aware of anyone who has a grudge against him?" It's an obligatory question; I'm just checking a box. I don't think this was about Nick at all; if he's innocent, then he was just a patsy to blame the shooting on. If he's guilty, then grudges against him are beside the point.

"No, I can't think of anyone. Nick's a good guy; everybody likes him."

"Did he talk to you about his job?"

"Sometimes. He was okay with it; he thought the people were nice. He wanted to make more money, but they turned him down for a raise."

I'm not happy to hear Duran say this, though the prosecution will find out about it anyway and claim it as a motive. It makes it less likely I'll call Duran as a character witness.

"Ever known him to be violent?"

"He got in a fight once, but he didn't start it. It wasn't that big a deal."

"When was this?"

Duran shrugs. "Not sure. More than a year ago. This other guy was drunk."

"Has Nick seen the guy since? If you know . . ."

"I don't think so. But really, it was a quick thing; I only men-

tioned it because you asked if I ever saw Nick do anything violent."

"The morning of the shooting, did you notice anything unusual at Nick's house?"

"What do you mean?"

"Anything at all. Maybe people around who you never saw
before?"

"No, but I leave really early for work."

I don't have anything else to ask Duran; I've gotten nothing
out of this interview, which is pretty much what I expected.

"Will you get Nick off?"

"I hope so."

"There is no way he did this. No chance. He didn't even own
a gun."

I think my ears actually, physically, perk up. "How do you
know that?"

"Because I told him we should each get one; we don't live in
the greatest neighborhood. But he wouldn't do it; he was afraid
of them. He said he'd probably shoot himself accidentally."

"Did you get one?"

"Damn straight I did."

The Castle Diner in Nutley claims it has the best hamburgers in New Jersey.

Not many New Jerseyans would agree with this dubious claim, unless they've led a mostly hamburger-free life. But the burgers are good enough, and burger judging is a subjective thing, so a diner can make any claim they want. In any event, the Castle was never lacking for customers.

Gerald Bullock ate at the Castle quite often. He certainly could have afforded better; Bullock was a top executive in a large office-supply company in Elizabeth, which sold its products as far south as Florida and as far west as St. Louis.

But the Castle was fine with Bullock; it felt more like home than home did. The magic had left the relationship between Bullock and his wife, Cynthia, and she had long ago stopped cooking for him anyway. They had both filed for divorce, mainly because she'd caught Gerald cheating on her, so he was going to be eating at the Castle for the foreseeable future.

On this night Bullock ordered his normal open-faced roast beef sandwich, with fries and a Diet Coke. He had long rejected the Castle burger claim; it was by no means the best even in Nutley. As always, he topped his meal off with a vanilla milkshake, defeating the purpose of the Diet Coke.

He lingered over the shake for a while, reading the newspaper as he sat there. As he was almost ready to leave, he started to feel strange. Then he felt a pain in his stomach that was excruciating, so much so that he fell to the floor, moaning.

The staff at the Castle was quick to react; they called 911, and the EMTs were on the scene within minutes. They stabilized him and quickly got him into an ambulance. In a short time they were at Montclair General Hospital.

The ER doctors initially were unsure what was wrong, but a series of tests determined that it was sepsis. Subsequent tests located the source of the problem as *E. coli* bacteria.

Bullock was admitted and put on fluids and antibiotics. He began to feel somewhat better and within hours was asking when he would be released. But the doctors wanted to keep him overnight, so his wife, Cynthia, was called, and she brought a change of clothes, toiletries, and a book that Bullock was reading.

The doctors assured Cynthia that there was nothing to worry about, so she went home.

At 4:04 A.M., Gerald Bullock lost consciousness and stopped breathing. Efforts to revive him proved futile, and at 4:11 he was declared dead.

Laurie tells me that Marcus is going nuts.

He hasn't gotten anywhere trying to use his street contacts to learn anything about the shooting, or about the kidnapping of Nick Williams. We have given him little to work with, which is why he insisted on being here today when Sam Willis presents his initial report.

Laurie asked me if it was okay, and I said yes. When Marcus insists on something, my programmed response is "Yes, Marcus, anything you say." I tell her that I haven't told Marcus yet about the fingerprint on the gun; I want to confront Nick first. I'm trying to figure out the best way to do that.

Corey Douglas is here as well and has brought along the only nonhuman member of the K Team investigators. It's his German shepherd, Simon Garfunkel, who worked with Corey when he was with the Paterson Police Department.

I'm glad Simon is here because Tara loves him and they play and wrestle together. Hunter tries to get in on it, but is usually relegated to watching. Sebastian thinks playing and wrestling are for suckers, so he sleeps through the whole thing.

They haven't invented the event that can keep Sebastian awake; he could sleep on the fifty-yard line at the Super Bowl. Actually, if he wanted to, he could even play; he's built like an offensive tackle.

Laurie is not the greatest cook in the world; she is the first to admit that. But somehow she was blessed with a talent for making pancakes; she is a pancake savant. Even she can't explain it.

But because of this talent, we wind up having a great many morning meetings at our house. Corey, Marcus, and Sam have no trouble downing ten each, usually leaving one for me.

When they are finally stuffed, we go into the den to talk. Sam has with him a large folder, and I immediately offer him the floor.

"Okay, let's start with Moore Law," he says. "As I'm sure you know, Jim Moore is no longer with us . . . he died three years ago. The firm has actually expanded considerably since then. They were only in three states when Jim bit the dust, and now they're in eleven.

"New Jersey was the first state; Jim was from here, born and raised, and this is where the home office is. In fact the main office was the one in Paterson that was shot up.

"I have the list of states the firm is now in; it's in the pages I'm going to give you. Steven Loomis is the CEO; he was Moore's top lieutenant and moved up when Jim left the scene.

"The firm basically deals in two areas, personal injury and medical malpractice. They are almost always the plaintiffs; if you are accused of a crime, they are not for you. I suppose if you're extremely wealthy, they would make an exception. But if you're extremely wealthy, you wouldn't want them . . . you'd want Andy.

"Personal injury can take any form: car, truck, or motorcycle accident, get run over as a pedestrian, slip and fall, you name it. It can also include illness as long as it is negligently caused—pesticides, asbestos, lead paint, et cetera. It's very lucrative.

"Medical malpractice is just what it sounds like and can also be extremely profitable. It can be a wrong diagnosis, a treatment mistake in the ER or in surgery, or an anesthesia error. If anyone in the world of medicine screws up, these guys are there to make them pay for it.

"In the last two years, the firm has won an estimated two and a half billion dollars for their clients, though because some settlements are confidential, it is hard to confirm the number. Not many cases make it to trial, maybe five percent.

"But medical malpractice in this country is huge, and getting bigger every year. And this particular law firm is all over it. Medical malpractice brings in about sixty-five percent of their revenue, and it's going up all the time. There's much more detail in the pages."

"What about the shooting victims?" I ask.

"I'm not quite finished with that yet, but what I know is in the folder. There was only one lawyer among the victims, a guy named Charles Brisker. He was forty-five, but had only been with the firm for almost four years. Brisker previously had an independent operation, but it struggled so he closed up shop.

"He was married for twenty-two years, grew up outside Boston, and went to Cardozo Law School. He has one daughter. If there was anything exceptional about him that would make him interesting to us, I haven't found it yet."

"Who was the client he was meeting with?" Corey asks.

"Gerald Stoneham. I'm not sure he was actually a client; he was a college friend of Brisker's, so maybe it was a social call. He is . . . was . . . an insurance executive with Quantum Care Insurance, so it's also possible it was a business thing. I'm finding out more about him."

"Nice work, Sam," I say. "All of this will help us kick-start things. What about the cell phones at Nick's house that morning?"

Sam smiles. "Saving the best for last. The GPS records are

inexact, as you know, but they can narrow the location to within forty yards. Based on that, there are two phones not belonging to residents that were there that morning at seven thirty. I'm talking about phones that left the area soon after and haven't returned."

"Whose were they?" I ask.

"One is owned by John McGuire. He's a plumber and was there for about an hour. I cyber-entered his company computer and learned that he was there to help one of Nick's neighbors with a hot-water issue. Seems legit."

"And the other one?" Laurie asks, getting slightly impatient with how Sam is drawing this out.

"Registered to a Ms. Elaine Attwood."

"This is the best you're saving for last?" I ask. "Who is Elaine Attwood?"

Sam smiles. "She's nobody; I can't find her anywhere, and the address that she has listed for the phone company is an abandoned house . . . hasn't been lived in for years. It's clearly a fake name."

"So we don't know the real name of the cell phone owner?" Laurie asks.

"Not yet. But I think we know where the person who owns it lives. The phone has been there on and off for weeks, including overnight. I have the address; it's an apartment building in Hackensack."

"Excellent. One more thing, Sam. I need to know where that phone went immediately after it left Nick's house."

He nods. "Won't be a problem."

I turn to Marcus. "Marcus, this is perfect for you. Work with Sam to follow the phone until you figure out who owns it. If it turns out to be a seventy-five-year-old retired librarian named

Elaine Attwood, don't confront her, and definitely don't shoot her. But if not, please let me know what you find out."

Marcus hasn't said a word the entire meeting and hasn't cracked a smile.

Until now.

was surprised that Steven Loomis was willing to see me.
As the CEO of Moore Law, he certainly wouldn't be sympathetic to the lawyer representing the accused shooter. Having five employees killed is a reason to hold a grudge.

But when I called him, he was actually receptive, and we are meeting in the Passaic office, which is at least temporarily his home base because of the shooting at the Paterson office. He had his main lieutenants under him in Paterson, with executives in each of the states the firm is in. But he sits at the top of it all.

"I appreciate your seeing me. It surprised me."

He looks puzzled. "Why?"

"You probably think my client is guilty."

"I do."

"He isn't."

He smiles, more condescendingly than I'd like. "That's what they have courts and trials for."

"You have a pen? I want to write that down."

Another smile. "Look, I want justice to prevail, and I only know you by your reputation. You're said to be annoying, and now I'm sensing that's an accurate assessment."

"Guilty as charged."

"Of course, I admit to being a bit cranky these days; nearly getting killed can have that effect."

"You nearly got killed?"

"That's how I see it. The only reason I wasn't there when the killer came in, when your client came in, is because it was a summer Friday and I was in Long Beach Island."

"Saved by a beach house."

He nods. "Anyway, I wanted to meet you; maybe after this is over I can hire you."

"I would rate that as somewhere between no chance and not in a million years."

"You can't be bought?"

"Not unless you're hiring me to play quarterback for the Giants, or shortstop for the Mets."

He shrugs. "Okay. You can't blame me for trying. And I'm going to need help. Charles and Monty were my two right hands."

"You had two right hands?"

"Yes. And now one of them is gone, and for all I know Monty, Sally Montrose, may not want to come back. Anyway, what can I do for you?"

The truth is that there is nothing I want from him; I am here to see how cooperative he will be. "Point me to another suspect."

"I beg your pardon?"

"Let's say Nick Williams didn't exist, and the police did not have a suspect. Who might your mind go to?"

"My mind would be a blank. I don't know, or at least I hope I don't, anyone who could do such a thing."

"Your firm has represented many people; surely some of them could be characterized as disgruntled. Maybe you didn't get them the settlement they anticipated and thought they deserved."

"Hopefully very few."

"Good; that narrows it down. Perhaps you could point me to those few disgruntled clients who were represented by the Paterson office."

He smiles. He seems to smile a lot at things that are not re-motely amusing. "So you want me to do your job for you."

"Absolutely."

"I'm afraid I can't do that, even if I wanted to, which I don't. I said I wanted to meet you, not participate in the defense. But if a client expressed displeasure to one of our attorneys, it would be privileged. I'm sure you understand that."

"What about the part where you wanted to see justice prevail?"

"I'll count on you to make sure that happens."

"Had you ever met Nick Williams?"

He nods. "Of course; I worked in that office."

"Ever heard anything negative about him?"

"You mean other than that he killed six people?"

"Other than that."

"No. I had never seen or heard any reports on him, positive or negative."

"Did you know the victims?"

"Obviously." He's starting to show annoyance. "I worked with all of them, but I was closest to Charles and Monty."

"Your two right hands."

"And fine attorneys. And fine people."

"Are you going to reopen that office?"

"No, we are not; that decision has been made. The survivors will be given as much time off as they need or want, and then they will work here in the new main office. Perhaps we'll reopen a Paterson office, perhaps not, but it won't be in that location."

"Just curious . . . why do you still tell people to 'call Jim'?"

"Continuity. It was and is a successful brand."

"Yet you expanded into a bunch of states where they never heard of him."

Loomis smiles. "They've heard of him now, or at least they had better, with our advertising budget."

"So a lot of people are calling Jim?"

"They are, but we're not mired in the past. I once read an analysis of the Disney Company over the years. Once the founder died, the company was struggling because whenever a crucial decision needed to be made, the executives spent their time trying to figure out what Walt would do.

"Then new, forward-thinking executives took matters into their own hands and the company took off." Loomis smiles. "So we don't spend much time wondering what Jim would do."

There is a frustrating limitation to the rules of discovery. The defense gets access to all evidence that the prosecution has, including interviews with their witnesses and potential witnesses. It's a breach if they fail to turn over everything, and that transparency is obviously a good thing, as long as they adhere to it.

However, in criminal cases, unlike civil litigation, we do not have the right to interview or depose those same people. We can make the request, but they are free to refuse. And since those people usually view us as the enemy, we get a lot of turndowns.

But we always make the effort, for two reasons. One is that we might get helpful information that goes beyond what the prosecution has. The other is the possibility that we can use something that they say in the interview to attack their testimony at trial. Lawyering is a contact sport.

I'm going to be visiting Nick at the jail later, but this morning I'll be attempting to contact some of these people. I'm preparing to use a substantial portion of the Andy Carpenter charm to get them to talk to me.

My first call is to Kathleen Brisker, wife of Charles Brisker, the lawyer killed in the shooting. This is not going to be fun.

A female voice says, "Hello?"

She sounds considerably younger than a person who might be

Brisker's wife, since the documents listed him as forty-five. "My name is Andy Carpenter. I'm trying to reach Kathleen Brisker."

"Andy Carpenter the lawyer?"

"Yes."

She hesitates. "Hold on." Then, "Mom!"

My keen deductive instincts tell me that this is the daughter of Kathleen and probably Charles. I hear more conversation in the background, but I can't make out what they're saying. It sounds like they're arguing.

After about forty-five seconds, the person comes back on the line. "She won't talk to you. I'm sorry."

"I understand." I give her my phone number in case her mother changes her mind. She thanks me and hangs up.

That went really well.

For my next trick, I call Sally Montrose, one of the two survivors of the shooting and the main witness against Nick. I'm expecting to be turned down "with extreme prejudice," but bizarrely, the opposite is true.

When I ask her if she'll meet with me, she says, "Am I allowed to?"

"Definitely." She's a lawyer so I'm surprised she doesn't know that, though she doesn't do criminal work. "But you're not required to; it's totally up to you."

"Okay, then, I think I would be willing to do that."

My charm is clearly more powerful than even I realize; it might actually fall into the dazzling category. We agree to meet for coffee tomorrow afternoon.

I think I want to end the morning phone calls on that high note, so I head down to the jail to talk to Nick. I haven't been here in a while, which I feel badly about. People in his position need to know that they are not being forgotten; sitting in a cell all day can do strange things to one's head.

As I arrive, Rafe Duran, Nick's friend and the other person Marcus is mentoring, is leaving. He sees me and asks how things are going.

"We're getting there," I say.

"I hope so. Nick is pretty anxious. I guess he should be, huh?"

I nod. "It's not easy, what he's going through."

Rafe nods his understanding. "Is there any way I can help?"

I tell him that at the moment there's nothing he can do, but I will contact him if that changes. He nods and heads for his car while I go inside and sign in.

Nick is brought into the interview room, his arms and legs again shackled. They're still being careful with him; this was no ordinary crime, so this is no ordinary inmate.

"Hey, Mr. Carpenter. It's good to see you. It's good to see anyone."

"Call me Andy. Have you had visitors?"

He nods. "Marcus has been here three times and Rafe was just here. Marcus says you're going to get me out of here."

Thanks a lot, Marcus is what I'm thinking. "Do you own a gun?" is what I say instead.

"No."

"How long has it been since you touched one?"

He thinks. "Maybe six months? Rafe has one, and when he showed it to me, I held it. Why?"

"They found the murder weapon down the block from you in a dumpster, with your prints on it."

He shakes his head. "Impossible. They're lying."

"No, they're not."

"Then I don't know how to explain it. I do not own a gun, and I did not kill my friends."

"How long was the ride from your house to where they kept you locked up?"

He thinks for a few moments. "I don't know that because I wasn't conscious. The ride back was to the rest stop on the parkway. I was blindfolded and laying on the floor in the back. It's hard to judge, but maybe forty minutes?"

"Why were you unconscious on the way there? Did they knock you out?"

"I don't know; I can't remember anything from the time I left the house until I woke up in that room."

"Did you have any bruises on your head when you woke up?"

"No. But . . ."

"What is it?"

"Now that I think of it, my arm was a little sore, like after you get vaccinated, you know? Nothing terrible, but I remember it."

"Good. That's helpful. Was there anything else you can remember about your time in that room?"

He nods. "One other thing, though it's minor. I told you there were two guys that seemed to be assigned to me, that brought me food. Only one of them talked, the big guy, and he kept calling me 'friend.'"

"Do you think you knew him?"

Nick shakes his head. "No, it wasn't like that. It was just the way he talked, at least that's what it seemed like. And he wouldn't answer my questions."

Nick doesn't remember anything else, so as all clients do, he asks me if we're making progress. I fend off the question; I don't want to depress him, but nor do I want to raise his expectations.

"How is Daisy? How is her leg doing?"

I smile. "I haven't seen her recently; I'm going to try and get there tomorrow. But Willie tells me she's doing great."

"Are you going to place her in a home?"

"Eventually; she's not ready yet."

He nods his understanding; this is not an ideal time for him to be adopting a dog. "Give her a hug for me. And a chest scratch; she loves that. She flops over on her back and looks like she's in heaven."

"I'll do that. It's a golden retriever thing."

I stand up, and he says, "Mr. Carpenter . . . Andy . . . I did not kill those people."

This morning I'm going to pretend I'm a regular person, not a lawyer.

It starts with taking Tara and Hunter for a long walk in Eastside Park. Sebastian still does not go with us on these treks; he prefers to slowly amble into the backyard to do his business.

Some dogs jump up eagerly when their human picks up a leash; Sebastian just snores. Like all dogs, he can't actually talk, but if he could, I suspect he would liken our Eastside Park walks to the Bataan Death March.

The media have pretty much stopped following me. Every once in a while a reporter will call and ask for an interview, but they've gotten the message that I've got nothing to say, at least until I have something to say.

When I get home, I have a quick breakfast with Laurie and then we have a FaceTime talk with Ricky, who is currently in Madrid with Rein Teen Tours. He sounds great, loving every minute of it, and even asks me how the football Giants are looking in preseason.

That's my boy.

I know he's having fun, but it makes me sad when he's not home. I must be getting soft in my old age.

Once we're off the phone, I head down to the Tara Foundation. I always feel guilty when I can't get there often because

I'm working on a case, but Willie and Sondra generally let me off the hook.

This time is no exception, and my mood is further uplifted by the dogs that are here. That they had been abandoned and faced an uncertain fate, but are now going to be assured loving homes, never fails to make me feel better.

I go into the back to see Daisy, still recovering from the broken leg. She has to remain relatively immobile, so she can't hang out with the other dogs. A wrestling match could break out and Daisy could mess up the progress her leg has made.

As Nick suggested, I scratch her chest and she flops down on her back to make my task easier. Her mouth opens in apparent delight. Nick was right; all dogs love this, but Daisy takes it to another level.

"How is the case going?" Willie asks, just before I leave.

"We're really just getting into it." He likes Nick a lot, so I want to manage his expectations. Willie thinks I walk on legal water.

"I still want to help, Andy. Whatever you need."

"Thanks; I know that."

The normal part of my day having reached its conclusion, I head for the Athens Coffee Shop on Broadway and near my office. I'm meeting a woman who is all too likely to send Nick Williams to jail for the rest of his life.

I had seen Sally Montrose's photo in the discovery documents, so I immediately recognize her in the back, sitting alone in a booth. She smiles slightly when she sees me and waves me over.

"Hello, Mr. Carpenter."

I say hello and sit down. A coffee cup in front of her has only a few drops left, indicating she's been here for a while. "I'm not late, am I?"

"No, I got here early. I find that these days I want to be around people; sitting alone in the house for some reason makes me anxious."

"You've been through an awful ordeal."

She nods. "Still doesn't seem real."

"I'm sure it must be hard to think about, and harder to talk about. So I really appreciate your meeting me like this."

"Actually, it helps to talk about it. And I . . . I sort of have a need to know why Nick would do something like this."

"Could you be mistaken?"

"About whether it was Nick? I wish I was. He was my friend, or I thought so. We talked all the time. I really liked him; everybody did."

"You didn't see his face?"

"No. But I saw the tattoo. And he called me 'Monty,' just like he always did. He was really going to shoot me . . . I just can't understand it. What he did to the others . . . ."

"Did you recognize his voice?"

"I think so . . . it was a very stressful situation. But he walked like Nick also, straight up; you've seen him, right?"

I don't respond to that since I have noticed that he walks in an erect position. "I can imagine how stressful it was." I'm very much feeling sorry for this woman. "Why do you think he spared you?" I know what she told the police; I just want to hear if the story has changed at all. Sometimes it does.

This time it doesn't. "I'm not sure, but it was probably Laura getting away. She was in the next office and she heard everything."

"Why was Laura in the next office? Isn't she a paralegal?" The discovery had said the paralegals had the smaller offices on the other side.

"We were working on a matter together, and the office next

to mine was empty, so she was working out of it temporarily. It was just easier." Then Sally asks, "Is there going to be a trial? Mr. Wallace said he wasn't sure, but that I should be prepared."

"I believe that there will be, yes. Nick swears that he did not do this, so he can't plead guilty."

"How could it not have been him?"

I don't have the answer to that, but I'm sure as hell going to have to come up with one.

It's been three days since I've heard anything about the person whose phone was at Nick's house the morning he was kidnapped.

That's about to change. When I get back from my morning walk with the dogs, Sam, Marcus, Corey, and of course Laurie are here and ready to give me a progress report.

It's going to have to wait for a while as Laurie is still making pancakes for her colleagues. In a few weeks, when Ricky is home, the majority of our work will be done in my office, and the pancake spigot will be shut off. We try to keep Ricky from hearing about our murder investigations, so that no one finds out and reports us to Child Welfare Services.

"I'm going to take you through it," Laurie says, when we're all seated. "We've accomplished quite a bit, but we're at the point where you have to provide direction."

"I am Andy Carpenter, Provider of Direction."

She frowns. "So I've heard. Anyway, Sam isolated the phone that was at Nick's house and was listed in the name of Elaine Attwood, to the Carlton House apartments in Hackensack.

"It took a couple of days of surveillance, watching people leave and return to the building, and matching it up with the movements of the phone. He was good enough to carry it with him whenever he left, so that made it easier."

"He?"

"Yes. Unless Elaine Attwood is about six-four, two hundred and fifty pounds, and mostly bald, it's not her."

"Do we know his name?"

"No, but we're getting there," she says. "I followed him into a diner and was able to get a water glass that he used after he left. I asked Gina Marinelli to get prints off it. She'll run the prints and get back to me if they get a hit."

Gina is a friend of Laurie's from her time at Paterson PD; she's in forensics. "Did you ask her to keep it to herself?" I ask.

"Of course, and she will. We also got a photograph of him. Corey went into the gym where he works out and took it secretly. It was a mostly male gym, and my coworkers were afraid I would attract too much attention in workout clothes."

She says it with obvious annoyance, but they were right. Laurie would attract attention if she were wearing a refrigerator freezer.

She takes out the photograph and shows it to me. I never saw this guy before and am not sure I want to see him again. In the picture he's preparing to lift a barbell that looks like it weighs more than Peru.

"If the print doesn't tell us who he is, maybe we can send this to Cindy and get her to run facial recognition," I say. Cindy Spodek is the number two agent in the Boston office of the FBI, and she's a good friend of Laurie's.

Laurie nods. "We can try that, but we should hear from Gina by the end of the day."

"Where else has our boy gone besides the gym and the diner?"

"So far nowhere," Laurie says. "Or at least his phone hasn't gone anywhere. We don't have eyes on the apartment building full-time."

"So what do you guys recommend?"

Laurie turns. "Corey?"

Corey says, "Nothing for the moment. Confronting him is unlikely to get us anywhere; we have more chance of watching him and following his movements, maybe see who he might meet with. Just because he hasn't done any of that so far doesn't mean he won't. When we learn who he is, I might feel differently, but for now I think we lay back."

"Marcus? You agree?" I ask.

He nods, though I'm sure he is itching to confront this guy.

"Okay, then we're all on the same page. Please keep me posted, and definitely let me know as soon as we have ID'd him."

"Will do," Laurie says. "But he's not our shooter. Body type is nothing like Nick; the witnesses could not have seen this guy, hood or no hood, and mistaken him for Nick."

I nod. "No doubt about that. But it will still be worth asking Sally Montrose if she knows him; I'll take care of that at the appropriate time."

"It will be a big help if she does," Laurie says. "We still have to establish a connection to that office. Not only did the shooter know his way around, but he knew enough to call her by her nickname."

The meeting breaks up and I am about to head into the den to reread the discovery documents when my cell phone rings. I don't recognize the caller ID number, and I hate talking on the phone in general, but I answer it.

"Mr. Carpenter?"

It's a young woman's voice that sounds vaguely familiar. "That's me," I say, because it is me.

"My name is Karen Brisker. We spoke on the phone the other day. You called to talk to my mom."

"Right . . . sure. Of course I remember. How can I help you, Karen?"

"Well, she wouldn't talk to you, and I'm sorry about that."

"It's okay. I understand."

"But I'd like to talk with you. I would like that very much."

Karen Brisker wanted to talk to me, but she had very specific ideas about where the talk would take place.

Actually, that's not entirely true. She was firm in where it would not take place, and those forbidden locations included my office, her house, and anywhere in public.

I suggested that I pick her up in Eastside Park and that we drive to a secluded location where we could talk in my car. That's why we are in the parking lot of the Bergen Town Center in Paramus, near the back where there are currently few other cars.

Karen is nineteen and a sophomore at Northeastern, majoring in sociology. She told me this as we drove, and it felt like a way to delay her getting to whatever is the subject at hand.

"I'm sorry about this secrecy," she says when we're parked. "I just don't want my mom to know I'm talking to you."

"No problem. I love going to department stores as long as I don't have to go inside."

"Shopping is not your thing?"

"I don't really understand how it could be anybody's thing."

"My boyfriend is the same way."

Time to get to it. "What did you want to talk to me about, Karen?"

She nods, understanding that there's no putting it off any longer. "My father, and the way he was before . . . before he died.

He was worried . . . scared. It's the first time I had ever seen him like that, even though he tried to hide it from me."

"What was he scared of?"

"I don't know, and Mom doesn't either. But he wanted us to go away for a couple of weeks, maybe down to the shore or to visit friends in California. I think he was afraid for our safety."

"And you think that what happened proves he was right?"

She shakes her head. "My mom says that it did, and I guess she's correct, but it doesn't fully make sense to me. If he was worried about that man coming in and shooting like that, he could have just called the police. This was something different."

"It sounds like you're right. Do you know who Gerald Stoneham is?"

"I read that he was the man killed in the office with my dad. I think I heard my father mention him once, but that was a long time ago. Maybe they went to college together?"

"But they weren't friends now?"

She shrugs. "Not that I know of, but that doesn't mean they weren't. My mother said she didn't even know him."

"Why won't your mother talk about all this?"

"I think she's scared for me. Whatever danger it was, it could still be out there. So she's putting her head in the sand; at least that's how I see it."

"But you're not doing that."

"No. If someone else killed my father, not the person they arrested, then I want them caught. I can't stand that they could get away with it."

I can see her eyes tearing up as she adds, "We had lunch together that day, and then a few hours later he was gone. There is so much I wish I could say to him now."

This is an impressive young woman, but I'm afraid if I say so, it will sound condescending. "I think you did the right thing coming to talk to me, and I promise no one will find out that you did."

"Should I go to the police?"

"You certainly can if you want."

"I'm afraid people will find out that I did."

"I have a friend; he's the head of the Homicide Division. If you want, I can arrange for you to talk to him alone. I can guarantee he would respect your confidence."

"Let me think about it. If I decide to speak to him, should I call you?"

"Absolutely. And you can call me anytime about anything."

"Thank you. I feel better that I did this."

Tara, the answer is in that office. We need to find out what was going on."

I think Tara can always tell when I'm in trouble on a case, because then I tend to talk to her more on our walks.

She's good to bounce ideas off because she's smart, she can see through me when I'm bullshitting, and she never tells me when I'm wrong. That's not entirely true; she doesn't speak, but her tilt of the head means I'm not making any sense.

Hunter pretty much stays out of it; he doesn't have the legal training that Tara and I do. But hopefully he's learning on the fly, or on the walk.

"I think Karen Brisker is right that it wasn't Nick shooting up the place that her father was worried about. But it had to be office related because the killer knew his way around and knew enough about Nick to frame him.

"My biggest problem, besides figuring out what the hell is going on, is the murder weapon with the fingerprints. My best guess is that when Nick was unconscious, they put his hands on the weapon. He could have been knocked out all day, so they could have done it after the shooting or maybe were careful not to smudge the print.

"But the problem is, I cannot get my theory before the jury because I have no evidence to present that even indicates there was a kidnapping."

Tara stops to take a piss, which indicates to me that she agrees, or maybe disagrees, with my theory. It could mean that she is pissing on my ideas metaphorically, or maybe her bladder is just full. Tara works in subtleties that are often hard to understand.

But I continue, "I'd also like to know why Brisker sent that memo asking people to stay later on that Friday than usual. It could be a coincidence, but if it is, it's one that got a lot of people killed."

Our conversation is interrupted by the ringing of my cell phone.

It's Sam. "I know where the phone went from Nick's house that morning. And it went there again that afternoon and a bunch of times over the next few days."

"Great. Meet me at the house in a half hour, and tell Laurie we're going for a ride."

"Me too? I can go?"

Sam is dying to see what he calls "street action." "Sure, Sam, but we're just going to check things out."

"Should I be packing?"

"No, Sam . . . we're not staying overnight. You don't even need to bring a toothbrush."

"I meant packing a gun."

"I know what you meant, and the answer is still no."

The dogs and I turn around and quickly head back to the house, something that would not have been possible in the days when Sebastian used to walk with us. Turning him around and getting him to move in the other direction was extremely difficult; he is the *Queen Mary* of dogs.

Sam and Laurie are waiting for me when we get back. I give out some dog biscuits, then the three of us are off in Sam's car.

"Where are we going?" I ask.

"It's out in Newton, west and north of here. Should take us under an hour."

That's consistent with Nick's feeling that the drive back was about forty minutes, though he couldn't be sure of it.

It actually takes us fifty minutes, and the GPS leads us to what looks like an abandoned warehouse or factory. No cars are around, and no other buildings within at least a quarter of a mile. If one was going to keep someone locked away, this would be an ideal place.

"No sign of life," Laurie says. "Let's check it out. Wait here."

Laurie gets out of the car, and I see that she is holding a gun, but keeping it concealed. As wives go, this one can be fairly intimidating.

She slowly walks around the building, looking in windows, but ready for whatever she might find. Eventually she comes around the other side and makes her way back to the car. "Come on."

"Can we get in?" I ask.

She nods. "There's a rear door with a weak lock; I'll shoot it off."

We drive around the back; this way we'll have the car nearby should we have to get out of here quickly. Sam turns out to have another talent I was unaware of; he takes out a pocketknife and picks the lock. Apparently it's not only computers that Sam can break into; he's also proficient at non–cyber entry.

The inside of the place is entirely empty; it looks like it might have been a factory of some kind, though I have no idea what they made here.

Along the outer walls are what looks like either offices or storage rooms. Laurie points. "Let's go in that one over there."

"Why?"

"Because there are black sheets over the windows; I saw them when I walked by."

We go toward that room, and the door is open. As soon as we walk in, it's obvious that Nick was in this room. There is a bathroom, as he described, and a large closed hook mounted into the wall. I would bet anything he was chained to it.

For a few moments no one says anything; we all know what we are looking at. Finally I say, "Get some photos of this, Sam. Laurie, can you have someone come out here to look for prints?"

"Of course," Laurie says, as Sam snaps away with his cell phone camera.

"Marcus was right," I say. "We've got an innocent client on our hands."

His name is Russell Wheeler," Laurie says. "There's a warrant out for his arrest in Chicago."

"On what charge?" I ask.

"Murder, and while there is only one charge, it is not considered an isolated event. Mr. Wheeler is a hit man, and a high-priced one at that. Here's a photo that the local police there are using."

The photo shows a man with a mustache and goatee, both of which he no longer is sporting. I guess it's his version of a disguise, and it might actually be effective, at least around here. People in New Jersey do not spend their day on the lookout for Chicago criminals.

"According to Sam, he's subletting the apartment directly from the owner, using a false name. But we haven't seen him do anything; his recent life has been confined to the apartment, the diner, and the gym."

"We need to provoke him."

Laurie nods. "That's what I was thinking as well. If we rattle his cage, maybe he'll lead us to his partners."

"Right. But I'm not sure *partners* is the right word. This feels like Wheeler is a soldier, waiting for his next assignment."

"What is our obligation here? Do we have to report his location? Wheeler is a wanted criminal." As an ex-cop, she has a higher ethical standard than I do. I understand and accept that;

if there was an ethical standards Olympic team, I would not be invited to try out.

"We have no legal obligation," I say because it's true. "We are not required to tell the police." When she looks skeptical, I add, "Trust me on this."

"I do. Now what about a moral obligation? He's a hired killer; what if he kills someone else? We could have prevented it by having him arrested."

"Laurie, if Wheeler were to disappear tomorrow, his bosses would not pack their things and go home. They would just hire someone else. Keep in mind that Wheeler was not the shooter; he's by far the wrong body type. And Nick said there were two guys who were holding him; the other was more his size."

"Okay," she says without much conviction.

"The greater good, morally and every other way, is that we do what we can to take down the entire operation. The shooter was not some lone wolf, a loser who sits in his basement collecting guns and spewing hatred on the internet.

"These are people who didn't bat an eye about gunning down all those people; if we don't take them down, they are not going to ride off into the sunset."

"You're right," she says. "So what do we do?"

"We shake up his world and see what that gets us."

"I'll call Marcus and Corey."

"We'll need Sam also; he's been monitoring Wheeler's movements."

The phone rings and Laurie answers it. After her opening "Hello," she just listens and finally says, "I understand. Thank you, Frank."

She hangs up. "No prints in the room where they held Nick. The place has been wiped clean."

"I'm not surprised, but Nick will be relieved to know we found the place."

I head down to the jail to see Nick and show him the pictures of the room. I do so as soon as he is brought in, and he is stunned by them. "You found it."

"We found it. It's almost an hour west of here."

He can't seem to stop staring at the photos. "I wondered if I'd ever get out of there." Then, "Does this help us? Does it prove what happened to me?"

"Not yet; we can't prove that you were there. And even if we could prove it, you could have gone there voluntarily. But we think we have a lead on one of the guys who took you. The big guy."

"Be careful. He is not a guy to mess with."

"Turns out neither is Marcus."

When plans are being made for anything that might involve violence or personal danger, I am a silent partner in this group.

Laurie and Corey, being ex-cops, along with Marcus, being Marcus, are in charge of the tactics to be used. I don't have to be silent; I could voice my opinions in a firm, decisive way, but they would ignore me, so why bother?

Sam approaches it differently. Since he considers himself a combination Eliot Ness and Batman, he is quick to voice his strategy ideas. Everyone completely ignores him as well, except for me. Occasionally I'll say, "Good thinking, Sam," even when it isn't.

We're meeting to discuss how we will confront Russell Wheeler, a task made more difficult by his lack of movement. At least so far, he has only left his house to go to the diner and the gym.

Both of those places are in populated areas. The gym is out because Wheeler goes there in the daytime, and we do not want any bystanders around when we make our move.

That leaves the diner, but unfortunately Wheeler always parks on the street near the front entrance. He generally finishes eating at about eight thirty, when it is dark outside, but the area around the diner is well lit.

"It's got to be when he gets back to the apartment at night," Corey says. "The lot is always crowded by then because most people are home for the evening. And he doesn't have an assigned space because he's subletting."

"So where does he park?" Laurie asks.

"Usually it has to be near the back, which is adjacent to a wooded area," Corey says.

"So we wait for him there."

Corey says, "There's always the chance that someone will be around, parking there at the same time, in which case we'd have to abort."

Laurie nods. "Understood."

They come up with a strategy for how to do it, and I am less than shocked to discover that it does not include a role for me. Even Sam has something to do; he is going to be outside the diner and will call to let us know when Wheeler is leaving.

It's a ten-minute drive from there to the apartment, so we can be in position when Wheeler arrives. The whole plan sounds risky to me, but I generally consider getting out of bed in the morning to be a crapshoot.

"So when do we go?" Corey asks, looking at me.

"The sooner the better."

"It's supposed to rain tonight," Laurie says. "Does that cut either way?"

Corey shrugs. "Hard to say. Maybe even less people will be around, and also they might be more prone to staying home. That helps in that the lot will be crowded, so fewer spots available. But it also might get Wheeler to look harder for a spot closer to the building."

"Worth a try anyway," Laurie says. "So let me ask a question. I know we're trying to scare him into making a mistake and revealing his partners, and maybe he will and maybe he won't. But what if he panics and runs, and we lose him? He's still got a warrant out on a murder charge. Don't we want him behind bars?"

"We do," I say. "And I've got an idea."

I leave the group to work out final details and call Pete Stanton. "I need to see you."

"So come down to Charlie's tonight. The Mets are playing the Dodgers."

"Now. It might result in you making an arrest of an actual guilty person, which would be a first for you."

He sighs. "All right. My office in a half hour."

I head down to the precinct and am ushered into Pete's office. "So what is this about?"

"In this country it's appropriate to offer a guest something to drink, maybe a diet soda."

"So I've heard. You going to tell me what this is about?"

"There's a guy named Russell Wheeler; he's a hit man out of Chicago who has a warrant out for his arrest on a murder charge. I have reason to believe he is in this area."

"Where did you get that reason?"

"It's confidential, and you interrupting is not helpful. I don't have access to him yet, but there is a point at which I might. I could then alert you and you can pretend you're a competent cop and arrest him."

"Hold on a minute."

Pete goes over to the computer on his desk and starts typing. I assume he's entering a database to find out what he can about Wheeler.

After five minutes, I say, "I'm getting bored and thirsty."

He doesn't answer, and three more long minutes go by before he gets up from the computer. "This is a dangerous guy."

"I'm aware of that."

"Does this have anything to do with the Nick Williams case?"

"I believe that would fall under the heading of 'none of your business.'"

"Call me when you know where he is, and be careful. You might even want to surround yourself with your buddies, especially Marcus."

"I cherish your advice."

I know that "scientists" might not agree, but nervous days literally go much slower than nonnervous days.

I'm not sure if it has something to do with the rotation of the earth, or the tides, or whatever, but when I'm anxious about something coming up, days can take thirty or even forty hours. Or longer.

Today is a perfect example. The eight hours between my leaving Pete's office and our getting in place to confront Wheeler have taken about a week, give or take a couple of days.

But the time has finally arrived. I'm sitting in the passenger seat of my car, and Laurie is in the driver's seat. Corey and Marcus are in Corey's car, about fifteen feet from us. We're both near the only open spaces in the lot, which is hopefully where Wheeler will park when he returns.

The call comes to my phone at eight forty-five, fifteen minutes later than expected. That's actually a good thing because by now it's fully dark. I call Corey and tell him that Wheeler is on his way. I then see Marcus exit the car.

I'll be able to watch and hear through my window, but I'll have no role in the first stage of what is about to take place. I can't say I'm sorry about that.

It starts raining much harder, the drops are pounding on the car. I see headlights coming toward us; I assume and hope it's Wheeler's car, but I have no way of knowing. He's going slowly, looking for a spot out here in the back, not closer to the building.

I guess he's not afraid of rain; let's see how he feels about Marcus.

Wheeler pulls in exactly across from our car; we couldn't have hoped for any better. He sits in the car for a short while; maybe he's hoping the rain will let up a little bit. And a few seconds later it seems to do just that. If all goes according to plan, that will be the last thing that will go his way tonight.

He finally gets out of the car and starts to move quickly toward the building; this is the first time I've seen him, and the reports are correct. He's a really big guy and little of it appears to be fat.

Corey and Marcus move toward him from opposite directions. "Hey, Wheeler," Corey yells, and Wheeler naturally turns toward him.

"You got a problem, friend?" Wheeler asks, not in a friendly way. Nick said the larger of the two kidnappers called him "friend" as well. It adds further credibility to Nick's story, though it's not needed. He is clearly telling the truth.

While he's talking to Corey, Marcus reaches him and either punches or elbows him in the side of the head. He goes down like he's shot. Hopefully we have the right guy, and this isn't some poor large slob whose wife is waiting for him in the apartment with dinner. But Corey has seen him before, so I'm assuming this is actually Wheeler.

Laurie starts the car and pops the trunk open. Marcus drags the unconscious Wheeler over to us by the collar and hoists him with apparently little effort, then dumps him into the trunk. This is a big guy, and Marcus picked him up like he was a small bag of shit, which he is.

Before closing the trunk, Marcus reaches in and frisks him,

coming up with two handguns. It's a smart move; we don't want a suddenly conscious Wheeler coming out of that trunk firing.

Marcus slams the trunk, and we're off. Corey and Marcus follow us as we drive to the Hackensack River County Park. It's a short drive, and Corey has scouted out a place down by the river that he is sure will be uninhabited at this hour.

If he's wrong, and there are people there, we will improvise. But I can't imagine anyone will be hanging out there in the rain at this hour.

Corey seems to have been right; it looks perfect for us. We both park down by the river, and Corey takes a bucket to the edge and fills it with water. He brings it back to the car and sets it down while Marcus opens the trunk. Laurie has her gun in one hand and her flashlight in the other, just in case Wheeler had a third weapon that Marcus missed.

The light comes on in the trunk and Wheeler is, as expected, still there. He is slowly starting to come to, but an impatient Corey dumps the bucket of water on him, hastening the process. I've got a hunch that river water is not exactly Evian . . . if there are living things in it, I'm going to set fire to this car and get a new one.

"Get out," Corey commands.

Wheeler is slow to react, so Marcus grabs him by the arm and pulls him out, leaving him on the ground. Laurie keeps the flashlight shining into his face, which must be both semiblinding and further disorienting.

"Welcome to the party, asshole," I say. It's a Bruce Willis line from *Die Hard* that I've always wanted to use. I've never had the opportunity, both because I go to few parties, and because I don't hang out with assholes.

"What's going on? Who the hell are you?"

"I'm your worst nightmare." That's a line from a *Rambo* movie; I'm on a cinematic roll here.

"You guys don't know who you're messing with," he says, regaining his bravado.

"Yeah, we're intimidated as hell. How was the ride in the trunk?"

He doesn't answer, so I add, "We know exactly who we are dealing with. You're Russell Wheeler. You and your low-life friends are responsible for the shooting at the law firm."

"That's bullshit."

"Russell, you're soaking wet and you've probably pissed in your pants. You're lying here on the ground; you were just unconscious in the trunk of our car. You think we're bluffing? You think we picked you at random? We know who you are and what you did."

I'm deliberately not mentioning the Chicago murder warrant. If he knows that we're aware of that, it might further prompt him to leave the area.

He doesn't answer, so I say, "So here's what's going to happen. You have twenty-four hours to agree to go to the cops and tell what you know. You'll get a deal, which is more than I can say for your friends."

"Kiss my ass," he says, getting to his feet.

"Did you get permission to stand up?"

He points to Laurie. "She puts that gun away and none of you will be standing."

I look at Laurie and she puts the gun away. Marcus steps forward.

"This is a friend of the guy who was blamed for the shooting. He doesn't like you. What are you going to do about it?"

Wheeler assesses the situation, but he's furious and humiliated and not thinking clearly. Or maybe he's not capable of thinking clearly on his best day.

In any event, he no doubt knows he's bigger than Marcus, so he throws a punch at him. It's a sharp, crisp punch; Wheeler obviously knows how to handle himself. It would be a more effective punch if Marcus were still in the place he was in when Wheeler started to throw it.

Instead, he's somehow six inches to the side; Marcus may even be quicker than he is tough. The old Muhammad Ali boast comes to mind: he would say he was so fast he could turn off the bedroom light switch and be in bed before it got dark.

Marcus is still within range to deliver a punch to Wheeler's midsection, which sends him back to the ground, writhing in pain and gasping for breath.

Marcus leans over; I think he's going to keep hitting him. I have mixed feelings about it.

"Marcus," Laurie says, and that is enough to get him to stop. Laurie has a way with words.

I look down at Wheeler and say, "Twenty-four hours."

We leave Wheeler in the park to get home on his own.

Sam has already attached a GPS tracking device underneath Wheeler's car. Between that and the GPS on his phone, we should be able to keep tabs on his whereabouts if he tries to run.

"Do you think he will?" Laurie asks.

"Hard to say. But he has to be worried; just the fact that we've ID'd him and tied him to the shooting must be bewildering. He must think he covered his tracks, yet here we are."

We settle down in the den with glasses of wine; it's my preferred way of decompressing after tangling with dangerous hit men. We sit on the couch and Tara jumps up between us, giving her the potential of having four hands petting her at once.

"You sounded like you were enjoying yourself," she says.

I smile. "I was, in a weird sort of way. The guy is a piece of garbage; even if we are one hundred percent wrong about his involvement in the law office shooting, which we're not, we still know he's a murderer. I liked watching him squirm and suffer, especially since between Marcus, Corey, and you I was invulnerable."

"But now you're vulnerable. We need to acknowledge that and deal with it."

"He doesn't know who we are."

"He'll figure it out. He'll read about the case and see your picture, if he hasn't already."

"Are you trying to spoil what has been a wonderful, romantic evening?"

"Never."

"Then let me spoil it. We still have no idea why those people were killed. We know that Charles Brisker was worried about something, or at least his daughter said so. But for all we know he could have been stressed about paying her college tuition."

Laurie shakes her head. "No. His daughter said he was worried about her safety and her mother's."

I nod. "Point taken." Then, "We know that Wheeler was involved because he took part in the kidnapping. But we don't know who he is working with, or what they are trying to accomplish. Which must be pretty important if it was worth killing six people for."

"We also know where Nick was taken to and held during those three days."

"Yes, but that doesn't help, at least not yet. First of all, we can't prove that he was there. Second, he's the only one who can describe what happened, and there is no way I am putting him on the stand. He would say he got kidnapped and the jury would just take his word for it? Richard Wallace would tear him apart."

She frowns, understanding the situation. "So what's our next step?"

"A few of them. You and Corey should try and use your cop connections to find out about Wheeler's time in Chicago, specifically who if anyone he associated with. I'll call Sam and ask him to do a deep dive on Charles Brisker, including what cases he's been working on in recent months."

"You said a few things. Is there a third?"

"Yes, we can keep a close eye on Wheeler and hope he's dumb enough to lead us to something."

"You think he will?"

I nod. "I do. I cannot imagine that he will have gone through what happened tonight and then head back to his apartment and just hang out. He has to be worried; he doesn't know what we might know about the shooting, but he has to be scared about it. Plus, this is a wanted guy who, if he's caught, could go to jail for the rest of his life. Doing nothing is not an option. That's why I gave him twenty-four hours; there is no chance he'd turn himself in."

"But how long do we give him before we turn him over to Pete?"

"Depends on how he behaves. The first thing I expect is for him to find a temporary place to live. The downside to our grabbing him at his apartment is that he knows it's not safe there."

"We had no other option."

"I know. It's not a problem; we can follow him wherever he goes."

"Here's a question," she says. "What is he doing here?"

"What do you mean? We believe he kidnapped Nick and was at least involved in the shooting at the law firm."

"I understand that; we know why he would have come here. But why is he still hanging around? He's a wanted killer who has just been involved in a huge crime. Is this the best place for him to be hiding?"

"Maybe his work isn't finished. Or maybe he's been put on hold in case he has to clean up any loose ends."

"Let's make sure you're not a loose end."

I hold up my wineglass. "I'll drink to that."

Even though I am confident that we can monitor Wheeler's movements through his phone and the GPS device on his car, I take it one step further.

I've asked Corey to position himself at the apartment building, so that he can physically follow Wheeler if and when he leaves there.

The main reason to have Corey physically following him is that if Wheeler meets with anyone, neither the phone nor the GPS device could tell us who that meeting is with. Corey can do that, and as an ex-cop trained in these things, I have full confidence that Wheeler will not know he is being tailed.

I told Sam I wanted an update on any phone calls Wheeler made by six o'clock this evening. I also asked for a similar update from Corey on any people Wheeler might see, but he'll call it in, so as not to leave his post.

All we can do now is wait.

Laurie has things to do; she's been shopping for Ricky's back-to-school stuff, getting his room ready, et cetera. He's coming home soon from his teen tour to France and Spain. Hopefully he's the same Ricky and doesn't want to eat foie gras instead of pizza or to become a bullfighter.

I alternate between going over the discovery documents and walking the dogs. Since I've read all the discovery, I reread things randomly; whatever I pick up is what I go over.

This time it's emails from Charles Brisker, including the one he sent asking people to stay late that day. The other emails do not reveal anything incriminating or relevant to our case, and I don't think I will ever know why he wanted the staff to remain past their usual leaving time on summer Fridays.

So it's off to walk the dogs. We've gone on three walks already today, and when I got the leashes out for the last one, even Tara looked at me like I was nuts.

Corey calls in at five thirty to say that Wheeler has left the apartment, suitcase in hand, and has checked into a motel in Garfield. It's one of those one-level buildings where you pull your car right up to the room.

Wheeler has had pizza delivered to the room, so Corey believes he is going to lie low for a while. Corey is confident that Wheeler has no idea that he was followed there. I tell Corey he doesn't have to stay there anymore.

Sam comes over at six to give us his update on Wheeler's actions since his humiliation last night. Sam's been monitoring Wheeler's phone calls and the GPS on his phone and the car.

"He moved," Sam says. "A few hours ago he left the apartment and went to the Colony Motel in Garfield, which is not exactly the Ritz-Carlton, but it's well off the beaten path. He hasn't left since he arrived there."

"Good." I don't bother to mention that I already know this from Corey. "What about phone calls?"

"Well, keep in mind that it's possible he made calls from a different phone than the one we know about. There could even be a landline in the apartment."

"Understood."

"He made three calls from the cell phone. The last one was to a local pizzeria in Garfield, so I doubt that's important."

"Probably not," Laurie says, getting frustrated with Sam's pace. He loves to drag these things out.

"The other two could be interesting. He made one call last night to a phone in Highland Park, Illinois. It's just outside Chicago."

"Who was he calling?"

"It was to a cell phone, but registered to a restaurant. No way to know who answered it."

"What time was this?" I ask.

"Nine thirty our time."

"That's about when we left him in the park," Laurie says.

Sam nods. "Right. That's where the phone was when he made the call."

"He wasn't ordering takeout from Illinois," I say. "What about the other call?"

"He called a phone in Short Hills; it belongs to a man named Derek Shaffer. I checked him out; he's an interesting character."

"How so?" I ask.

"He is a doctor, or at least he was one. He lost his medical license almost eight years ago when he was suspected of writing multiple digital prescriptions around the country for opioids."

"What does *multiple digital* mean?" Laurie asks.

"I don't know the amount of them, but you can be sure it was a lot if it came to the attention of law enforcement. As for the digital part, he accessed the pharmacies online and inputted the prescriptions. Pretty smart."

"How was it resolved?" I ask.

"Hard to be sure, but it seems like they didn't have enough conclusive evidence to go to trial. It appears they dropped the investigation in return for his agreeing to give up his medical license. Since then he has opened a medical consulting company;

I'm looking further into that, but he has very significant protections on his data."

"You can't break in?" I ask, barely concealing my surprise. Sam can get into anything.

"Not so far, but I haven't given up."

"Okay, thanks, Sam. We need to figure out what to do with all this."

"One more thing," Sam says. "I checked on cases that Charles Brisker worked on the past few months."

"And?"

"There's a lot of them; it was a busy office. I count forty-one altogether, but it's not all Brisker. They seem to collaborate a lot, so Brisker did not handle everything in each case."

"Forty-one?" I'm not pleased to hear this number; we do not have the manpower to dig into all of it. "Were some much bigger than the others?"

"Yes. There was a car accident victim, a rear-ender, that settled for six hundred grand. The victim broke three vertebrae in his neck. Then there was a claim against a builder who built some poor couple's house on what became a sinkhole; it settled for seven hundred grand.

"The biggest was a medical malpractice against Montclair General Hospital. Guy was admitted for sepsis; it was considered treatable, but he then died when he was prescribed the wrong meds. They were going to trial, but at the last minute the insurance company settled for two million two."

"And Brisker had a big role in each one?"

"He did."

"Can you get me the names of everyone involved in those cases?"

"Sure."

"Thanks, Sam. Laurie, you guys check these cases out. I'll take the big one, the medical malpractice two-million-dollar case."

"Okay. What are we looking for?"

"I have no idea. But let me know if you find it."

"Should I keep monitoring Wheeler?" Sam asks.

"Might as well, but it won't be long. We're going to pull the plug on this guy."

Laurie is amazing; she can talk people into anything.

It's remarkable what obvious decency, sincerity, and human kindness can accomplish; I just wish I could fake it well enough. But it doesn't really matter because Laurie works on my behalf. It's like having an interpersonal genie.

Just this morning she has gotten two people to talk with me, people that would probably have hung up the phone if I had called them. One is Laura Schauble, the paralegal who escaped the shooting, but who is a witness against Nick.

The other is Cynthia Bullock, whose husband, Gerald, died in Montclair General Hospital. Six months ago she hired Moore Law to file a malpractice suit, which was handled by Charles Brisker, and which resulted in a seven-figure settlement.

But both of those conversations will have to wait until tomorrow, because today I'm dealing with Russell Wheeler.

I called Pete to set it up, and the conversation started off with our typical warmth. "What the hell do you want?" he asked.

"I'm trying to save your job, on behalf of all defense attorneys who want to keep cross-examining you in the future."

"You have Wheeler?"

"On a silver platter."

"Where is he?"

"Some conditions."

Pete sighed. "Here we go. Let's hear them."

"One is that I'm there to watch it go down. And two is that you intensely question him about the shooting that you wrongly arrested Nick Williams for."

"You saying he was the shooter?"

"No, but he knows who was, and he helped set Nick up."

"What does that mean?"

"Here comes the last condition, and if you violate this, you will pay for every beer for the rest of your life. You are not to share what I am about to say with anyone. I may need to use this at trial, and I want it to be a surprise."

"Let's hear it, and then I'll decide."

"No, you'll make the promise now, or I will let Wheeler ride off into the sunset."

Pete thought for a few moments. "Okay."

"Wheeler and another guy, whose name is unknown, kidnapped Nick and held him prisoner for three days, so it would look like he ran. They hung him out to dry."

"Bullshit."

"Fact. You can use it in your questioning of him, but you don't share it with anyone."

"Okay. Now where the hell is he? By the time you tell me, he'll be in a rest home."

I told him, which is why I am now sitting in my car across the street from the Garfield motel where Wheeler is staying. Pete has at least a dozen cops assigned to this, including a SWAT team. There's no great reason for me to have insisted that I be present, except I have a desire to watch Wheeler go down. It will be entertaining.

Pete and his team are extremely professional about it, approaching the room from all different directions. Wheeler is about to get nailed, there's no question about that, and if he resists, it's not going to end well for him at all.

It's hard for me to hear anything from my distant vantage point, but I assume someone yells out a command to go, because suddenly they converge and kick in the door. They enter, guns raised, and I can hear shouting.

What I don't hear is any shooting, and that's a good thing. I don't care about Wheeler's health, but I would like him alive to at least maintain the possibility of a confession. And of course I don't want any cops hurt.

Since the operation seems to be over, I get out of my car and start walking toward the motel.

As I approach the room in question, I'm stopped by a cop. "No one goes further than this."

"I'm the reason you're here."

"No one goes further than this."

I'm about to argue the point when Pete comes out of the room, sees me, and walks toward me.

"You got him?"

"We found him, but someone else got him."

"What does that mean?" I'm afraid I already know the answer.

"He's dead. One bullet in the forehead."

I am obviously responsible for Wheeler's death, which fails to leave me heartbroken.

But it's true; I don't see any other way to read it. He clearly told his bosses about what happened, and that we were on to him. They responded not by providing him the help he sought, but rather by killing him.

He became a loose end that required "cleaning up."

It says a few things to me. One is that we are dealing with incredibly ruthless people, although the mass shooting at the law firm had already made that obvious. Two is that Wheeler was not important to the conspiracy; he was not an "upper-level" guy. He was a rank-and-file soldier and therefore totally expendable.

Three is that his former colleagues, now his killers, are professional and extremely dangerous, especially now that they must be aware that we are starting to unravel their plot. Wheeler was not a pushover; he was a trained killer who had survived in that world for a long time. He was also a wanted criminal who had managed to stay ahead of his pursuers.

But he wound up dead in a motel room with a bullet in his head.

His phone emerges from this as a key piece of evidence and potentially helps us in two ways. One is that we already know the two phone calls he made after we took him to the park. It stands to reason that one of those calls triggered his murder.

The other way in which the phone could be invaluable is in trial. If the phone was still in the motel room with Wheeler, then Pete and his forensics people would have confiscated it. That would tie it to Wheeler, and we could show at trial that the phone was at Nick's house the morning of the shooting. We can also show it went to the place where Nick was held, lending substantial credibility to his story.

There is always the chance that Wheeler's killer took his phone; it would have been the smart thing to do. I can't ask Pete because I don't want to draw attention to it.

A murder of a professional hit man wanted in Illinois is not likely to provoke an intense investigation by the Paterson police. They'll look at it, but not too deeply; then they'll just ship the body back to Illinois and let the police there worry about it.

But even if the cops here have the phone and check to see what calls were made, it's not a big problem for us. I don't mind them covering the same investigative ground as we do; maybe with their powers of enforcement they'll get somewhere that we can't.

More likely, they'd note the calls but not follow up on them; either way we're okay. The only crucial thing is that they have the phone.

Between the connections Laurie and Corey have to the Paterson PD, we'll be able to learn whether the phone was retrieved and made its way into the evidence room. I'm sure they can do so without calling undue attention to our interest in it. We need them to because we won't be getting the information in discovery. The prosecution would have no idea it's related to the Nick Williams case.

In the meantime, we have to dig deeply into those two phone calls; one of them has the potential to reveal who walked into the Moore Law office and killed six people.

I've got some interviews scheduled today, the day after Wheeler was found, so I ask Laurie to get the whole team together at our house this evening. I suggest a pizza dinner for the gang, and hopefully she'll see the merit in that.

In the meantime, I head to Montclair to see Cynthia Bullock. Her husband, Gerald, died in Montclair General Hospital. She subsequently won a malpractice suit, with a settlement of more than $2 million.

Laurie didn't tell her that I was representing Nick, just that I was a lawyer and that I wanted to talk to her about Moore Law. Laurie said that Cynthia was initially hesitant, but she turned out to be more curious than anything else and agreed to see me.

Sam has given me some background on the Bullocks. Gerald was a high-level executive at an office-supply company, while Cynthia has no apparent employment record.

They lived in a modest home that Cynthia has since sold for $310,000. She's moved into an expensive home in Montclair, which she could obviously afford to do with the ample settlement she received, as well as the money she made from her own house sale.

Sam also found that a mutual filing for divorce was pending and had not yet been granted. Obviously that filing is now as dead as poor Gerald.

Cynthia didn't want to meet me at her house, since she doesn't know me, so she said we could grab coffee a few blocks from where she lives. She specified a Starbucks in a shopping mall.

When I arrive, I see a woman that might or might not be her, already sitting at an outdoor table. "Mrs. Bullock?" is my clever opening line, and when she nods, I've got a hunch it's her.

I tell her I will go inside and get us coffee, and she asks for a nonfat, no-fizz, double-shot venti latte with three stevias, an obvious effort to humiliate me in front of the Starbucks employees. But I go in and get it, as well as a black coffee for myself, and bring it outside.

"Thanks for seeing me."

"You're representing that killer. I only found that out by searching your name online. Had I known, I wouldn't have agreed to meet you."

"If it's any consolation, I think the jury will find that my client is not the killer. But in any event, I don't have any questions for you about that incident."

"Then what is this about?"

"Your husband."

"That's even worse."

I nod. "I know, and I'm sorry for your loss. I'll try and make it quick."

"Please do."

"As I understand it, he collapsed and it was determined to be *E. coli*?"

"Yes, and no one could figure out what caused it. To this day they do not know why it happened. Gerald was incredibly fit and healthy; he ran marathons."

I don't bother telling her that bacteria like *E. coli* couldn't care less if their target runs marathons. "So he was taken to Montclair General as an emergency?"

"Yes, an ambulance was called and he was taken there. He was admitted, and within twenty-four hours he was dead. They killed him."

"How did they do that?"

"By giving him antibiotics that he was allergic to, that they knew he was allergic to."

"How did you come to turn to Moore Law for representation?"

"Because of all the advertisements. I didn't know one lawyer from another, but I thought if they could spend all this money on advertisements, then they must be doing well. And if they were doing well, then it was because they made money for their clients."

"Makes sense. So you just called their general number?"

"Yes, and they assigned me to a lawyer."

"Charles Brisker."

"Yes, it is so awful what happened to him. Such a sweet man, so empathetic. He was a pleasure to deal with."

"Did you talk to anyone else there as the case went along?"

"Yes, a number of people called me with questions or updates, but it was basically Charles who was my contact and the man handling things for me."

"And you eventually settled."

"Yes. It seemed like it was going to trial, but one day Charles called me with the good news."

"Was there anything about their representation that you found strange, or that you were dissatisfied with?"

"Nothing. They were very professional and transparent throughout the process. I kept pressing Charles for news, and he was very patient. I did not want that hospital to get away with this."

"I'm glad you were pleased," I say, wanting to get out of here. I have accomplished absolutely nothing except learning what *no-fizz* means.

"I wouldn't say pleased. I will miss Gerald every day for the rest of my life."

I don't mention that with the impending divorce filing she was going to miss Gerald every day anyway. Instead I say my good-bye and get the hell out of here.

A man is sitting in a dark green SUV in the parking lot, from where he can see the outdoor Starbucks tables, should he be so inclined.

I think I also saw him there when I pulled up, as I was looking for a spot. I remember wondering if he was going to pull out and I could take his space, but it soon became obvious that he wasn't going anywhere.

Laurie has taught me to be paranoid about these things, usually with good reason. She also preaches that I should trust my gut instincts, but generally speaking, few guts have worse instincts than mine.

I walk past him on the way to my car, but do not make eye contact. I'm not a big eye contactor anyway, and certainly not with people I might have reason to be afraid of.

I try to get a look at his face without making that eye contact, but it's hard because the eyes are part of the face. But I do the best I can and manage well enough to know that I don't remember ever seeing this guy before.

What I should do is take a picture of him on my phone, which would risk him seeing me do it. Despite that, I would have the courage to take it, if I were an entirely different person.

So the plan I come up with, such as it is, is to leave the parking lot and drive around for maybe ten blocks or so. If he's not following me, or if I can't tell either way, I'll drive back to the mall lot and see if he's still there.

So that's what I do. I won't call Laurie and ask for help or instructions until and unless I confirm that he's following me, which I doubt. I drive the ten blocks, and I don't see him anywhere behind me. I'm pretty sure that I would if he were there, but since I can't be positive, I head back to the lot.

I enter the lot and drive behind where he was, and I'm relieved to see that he's still there. But then I see something else that surprises me a great deal: Cynthia Bullock is standing alongside his car, talking to him through the window.

I don't want them to see me, so I note the license plate and get the hell out of here. I call Sam Willis and ask him to run the license plate; he can do that with no problem. Then I call Laurie and tell her what happened.

She's concerned that he might now be following me, but I assure her that he isn't, and that we'll talk about this new development tonight at our meeting.

I'm not at all sure that what I saw was in any way meaningful. The most likely explanation is that Cynthia has a friend, or boyfriend, who drove her to the mall and was waiting to drive her home.

The only thing that makes that possibility less likely is that she was at the driver's-side window, talking to him. If she was going to get in the car for a ride home, it would make no sense to talk to him standing on the driver's side. And it was a good while before I got back to the parking lot; she had plenty of time to get in if she was going to.

Even had this not happened in the parking lot, something about Cynthia Bullock bothered me. She showed absolutely no curiosity about why I was asking her those questions.

Her husband had died, she had made a fortune in a settlement, and now a strange lawyer was questioning her about it. These were obviously major events in her life, yet she never once asked me what my interest in them were.

That she knew about my representing Nick made her lack of curiosity even more surprising. What could her case possibly have to do with a mass shooting? Most people would have wondered about that and may even have been concerned about it. But not Cynthia Bullock; she just answered my questions and blandly moved on . . . to the guy in the SUV.

For now I have to move on to another meeting that has little chance of being productive. But it's information gathering and will help me to be prepared for what Richard Wallace is going to throw at me.

Laura Schauble lives not far from me in Paterson, just ten blocks away. I'm on Forty-second Street off Nineteenth Avenue, and she is on the corner of Thirty-third and Eighteenth. I walk past her house occasionally with Tara and Hunter when we're not going the Eastside Park route.

Schauble worked as a paralegal and was in the office next to Sally Montrose when the gunman was about to shoot her before getting distracted by something. She told the police that she also believed the killer was Nick Williams.

Once we're settled in her den, she says, "I've seen you walking your dogs very often."

I smile. "They do like to walk."

"They're beautiful."

"Thank you." This is obviously a smart woman. "Tell me, what exactly do you do at the firm?"

She smiles. "Nobody does anything 'exactly'; it's a very collaborative situation. Everybody works together. But I do typical paralegal stuff; I'm sure you know what that grind is about. I'm also the informal bookkeeper. I have some accounting in my background."

"What does that mean, you're the informal bookkeeper?"

"Well, we had . . . have . . . an outside firm that does all the HR stuff and payroll, so I dealt with them when issues came up. It didn't take a lot of my time."

"So there was no CFO?"

"Not for a long time. The important financial matters were handled by Mr. Loomis and Mr. Brisker. I'm not sure why I'm referring to them this way, you know, as Mr. Loomis and Mr. Brisker. They were always Steven and Charles. It was a very informal atmosphere; not what I would have expected in a law firm."

"When you say the important matters, does that include things like paying out settlements?"

She nods. "Yes, Mr. Brisker directed that. He would instruct the banks on the wire transfers."

"Is that for all the offices, even in other states?"

She nods. "Yes, they all came through the main office . . . our office." She smiles a little nervously. "I guess you want to ask me about that day. Can we get that over with? I don't like talking about it."

"I understand and I'm sorry. I'll try to make it brief. I know you've told everything to the police, but could you just describe what happened as you saw it? Please don't leave anything out."

She nods and takes a deep breath; it is not the kind of thing one wants to relive. "I was in the office next to Monty's . . . that's Sally Montrose. We were working on a case together; she was the attorney and I was the paralegal helping her. I was at the file cabinet, so where Monty was she could not have seen me, and I couldn't see her."

"That wasn't your regular office?"

Laura shakes her head. "No, it was empty, at least for the time being. The firm had hired another lawyer, and that person was going to start the Monday after the . . . after that horrible day. It was going to be his office. For the time being Sally had some file cabinets moved in there; we were working on a case together. She thought it would be easier."

Laura gets a strange look on her face and I ask her what's wrong.

"I just realized that if Sally hadn't told me to work out of that office, I'd have been back with the others. It saved my life."

I want to get her back on track, so I prod her with "So you were at the file cabinets in the adjacent office . . ."

"Yes. I heard some strange noises, but I didn't think much of it. I started to walk towards the door between the offices when I heard someone say, 'Sorry, Monty.' Then I saw the gun in his hand, and I turned and ran." Laura smiles with some embarrassment. "It was not my finest moment."

"It was completely understandable. Did you recognize the voice?"

She shrugs. "I think so. It sounded like Nick, but I can't be sure. But I did see the hook tattoo on his arm. And I saw one of his sneakers, with those stripes on them."

"Did whoever it was run after you?"

"I don't think so, but I don't know for sure. I didn't turn around. I ran through the back door and out into the street."

"Was the back door open?"

"Yes."

"Did you see anyone out there? Maybe a car in the alley?"

She thinks for a moment. "Yes. I think so. Yes, because I considered hiding behind it, but instead I kept running."

"Was there anyone in the car?"

"I don't know. I really didn't look."

"You usually left early on Fridays? But you didn't that day."

"Right. Charles had sent an interoffice message asking us to stay late; there was to be a meeting that he described as important."

"But you don't know what it was about?"

"No. Now I guess I'll never know."

"Have you gone back to work?"

She shakes her head. "No, I'm not sure I ever will, at least not there. I think I need to get away from it. I'm trying to figure it out now."

"I understand. Did you know Nick well?"

"Yes, that's what makes this so strange. He was so nice and friendly; it's all so hard to wrap my head around."

"Maybe things are not what they seem."

"I hope not. But I do want whoever did this to be caught." Then, "They told me I will have to testify."

"You'll be fine. Just tell the truth."

Laurie has a bunch of pizzas waiting when I get back from walking Tara and Hunter.

Corey, Marcus, and Sam have also arrived; I think they were drawn by the smell of the pizzas. The pies are from Patsy's, which makes them serious contenders for best pizza in the universe.

Laurie is secure in the knowledge that no one will attempt to take any of her pizza. That's because she orders them covered with vegetables, in this case artichokes and broccoli. I hate to use the words *pizza* and *disgusting* in the same sentence, but there is no other rational way to describe it.

The rest of us chow down on the normal pizzas, and when we're finished, we break out the beer, wine, and diet sodas and go into the den.

I start it off. "As you know, Russell Wheeler is dead. I don't think that calls for a moment of silent reflection; the guy was a killer. I don't believe there is any doubt that our dealing with him the other night set off a chain reaction that ended in his death. To think otherwise would be to believe it was a ridiculous coincidence. When it comes to matters like this, I don't believe in any coincidences, and certainly not ridiculous ones.

"There were no indications we were watched that night, and I'm sure nobody in this room went around bragging about it. So Wheeler must have said something about it in the short time between our leaving and his taking a bullet in the head.

"We know that he made two phone calls after we questioned him. It's obviously possible that he had other contact with people, maybe on a different phone, but we have no knowledge of it. So all we can do is assume that it is one of those calls that got him killed. Sam, please tell them what you told me about the calls."

So Sam does that, describing the call to the restaurant/bar in Highland Park and the call to the former doctor turned medical consultant in Short Hills.

"So we need to dig into both situations, and we need to do it fast. Before we know it, we'll be in trial, and we had better have someone to point to as a possible perpetrator besides Nick. That jury is not going to be happy unless they have someone to blame for six deaths."

"Someone is going to have to go out to Highland Park," Corey says.

"I agree; thanks for volunteering. I also think Sam should go with you."

Corey doesn't look happy about that, but I think Sam is about to give me a high five.

"I can handle it," Corey says.

"I'm sure you can, but it will be easier with Sam there. You might have to do some tracking of the phone; that's the only lead we have as to who Wheeler called."

"Okay," Corey says, understanding my logic but still not happy about it. I'm sure he is envisioning having to curb Sam's desire to be a gun-toting private eye.

"Great. Now let's talk about Derek Shaffer, our doctor, or ex-doctor, in Short Hills."

"I've got some interesting information on him," Sam says.

"Good," I say. "Interesting information is always welcome."

"His consulting company is called Shaffer Medical Consultants, not the most creative name he could have come up with. I'm still unable to penetrate their online firewall."

"Please tell me that's not the interesting information," I say.

"No. You know the license plate you gave me to trace? The one from that mall?"

"Of course. Sam, land the plane, will you?"

"About to touch down right now. That car is registered to Shaffer Medical Consultants."

"That definitely qualifies as interesting information, and it makes it clear that Cynthia Bullock was not just chatting with a friend when she was standing at that car. Do you have a photograph of him?"

Sam nods. "Hold on." He takes out his phone and starts pressing buttons. Sam presses buttons on his phone with the speed of the average fifteen-year-old, which is to say he is lightning fast.

After about twenty seconds, he hands me the phone with a picture of Shaffer on it.

"It's not the guy in the parking lot," I say. "Shaffer is at least fifteen years older."

"We need to pressure Shaffer," Laurie says. "Whatever is going on, he's neck-deep in it."

"I agree. Let's start the process." I pick up the phone and call Eddie Dowd and tell him I want a subpoena sent to Shaffer, alerting him he will be called to testify as a defense witness in the Nick Williams trial.

"Let's see how he reacts to that," I say.

Ricky is coming home today.

Let me rephrase that to more accurately convey my feelings about this . . . *Ricky is coming home today!*

Laurie and I are at Newark Airport waiting for his plane to arrive from Madrid. Just his being old enough to be on a plane coming from Madrid is amazing to me. I'm obviously fine with him growing up; it's the speed at which he's doing it that I'm having difficulty with.

We've done this airport thing before; last year he went on a Rein Teen Tour of the American West, and it worked out perfectly. I'm not quite sure how they do it; I have one teenager and have my hands full when we go anywhere. They have planeloads of them and it seems to run like clockwork.

Once again this year he went on the trip with his best friend, Will Rubenstein, so Will's parents are here as well. We're all nervous, but not as anxious as last year. I think we're maturing.

The plane lands, which is always a positive development, and fifteen minutes later Laurie is suffocating Ricky in a massive hug. I go next, and I'm only slightly more reserved. That he is putting up with these hugs is yet another positive development.

The Rein people confirm that we are his parents and that he's not hugging some strangers, and we're good to go. We go with Will and his parents to lunch at the kids' favorite diner.

They go on and on about how great the trip was and how much

they saw, and I'm relieved that neither of them asks for a wine list.

All is good.

We head home and Ricky lights up when he sees the dogs. They seem just as happy to see him, and a lot of hugging and playing goes on. Even Sebastian stands up and wags his tail, which is the canine equivalent of me running a 10K.

Ricky asks me to play him in a game of *Madden Football.* "I haven't played a video game in two months," he says, as if there could be no worse deprivation.

He obviously wants to ease into it by playing a person well beneath his talents, and I am the perfect choice for that. I have never beaten him in a video game, not once; the kid was born with a joystick in his hand.

He beats me 31 to 7. I'd love to play another game to further boost his confidence, but real life intrudes and I have to go to a meeting.

I head down to Montclair General Hospital to meet with the hospital administrator, Dr. Amanda Clayman. In the small-world department, Clayman's husband, Bobby, was a teammate of Eddie Dowd's at Penn State. Eddie was a tight end, and Clayman was a linebacker. So Eddie set up this meeting for me.

I'm ushered into her office when I arrive and accept her offer of a Diet Coke. "Did you play football also?"

"No, but I occasionally bet on it."

"When Bobby and Eddie get together, that's all they talk about; it's like they're back in the locker room, or on the practice field."

"Sports has that effect."

She nods. "It does. And for a little while they forget they have arthritis in their knees." Then, "So I understand you want to talk about the Bullock case."

"Yes."

"We did not cover ourselves with glory."

"Can you describe what happened, from your point of view?"

She nods. "I can, only because all of it is in the court filings, so I am not breaking any confidentiality. Mr. Bullock was brought in to the ER suffering from an ailment which was quickly determined to be sepsis. Sepsis is basically an infection which triggers a reaction throughout the body. It can be quite serious; at its worst it causes organs to shut down and can be fatal."

"What caused it?"

"At the time we didn't know; we took a culture to determine the nature of the infection. Ultimately we discovered that it was *E. coli* bacteria."

"Would it have been life-threatening in this case on its own?"

"You never know, but very unlikely. Mr. Bullock was a fairly young man who was otherwise healthy. In almost all such cases the disease can be successfully treated with antibiotics. We immediately put him on medication, with terrible results."

I basically know what happened; I just want to hear it from her.

"Mr. Bullock was allergic to penicillin and all drugs within that family. It was clearly noted on his handwritten chart, and he verbally confirmed it when admitted. Yet one of those drugs, piperacillin-tazobactam, was inexplicably administered to him."

"And that killed him?"

She nods. "It caused anaphylaxis, which can be terribly serious and life-threatening in and of itself. Coupled with the underlying sepsis, it sent him into a crisis from which he could not recover, despite all our best efforts. An unspeakable tragedy."

She seems emotional just describing it; it is literally the opposite of what hospitals are about. When we met, Cynthia

Bullock had been considerably less emotional in describing the same events, even though they led to her husband's death.

"Did you determine who was at fault?"

"It was human error; let's just say that. The information was entered incorrectly into the computer and then was naturally assumed to be correct. We have instituted additional checks to make sure something like this cannot happen again."

"So you felt you had to settle?"

"That's really an insurance company decision, and in terms of the hospital above my pay grade. But we were clearly at fault, and that was reflected in the settlement."

"Who was the insurance company?"

"Quantum Care Insurance."

Wow.

When Charles Brisker was killed, he was meeting with an old college friend, Gerald Stoneham.

Stoneham, who was also killed, was an insurance executive with Quantum Care, the same company that settled the Bullock medical-malpractice case.

Did I mention I don't believe in coincidences?

Our focus at this point has narrowed down to two main areas, which seem connected.

One is the Bullock malpractice case. Charles Brisker handled it, it was an enormous moneymaker for him and Moore Law.

But he was worried about something, probably business related, to the point that he wanted his wife and daughter to leave town. Then he died in his office with a friend who was an insurance executive at the company that paid out the Bullock settlement.

Cynthia Bullock, grieving for the husband she was about to divorce, profited hugely from the case. And she represents a link of sorts to the other focus of our investigation . . . Russell Wheeler.

We know that Wheeler was one of Nick Williams's kidnappers. We also know that before he was himself murdered, he made two phone calls. One of them was to an unknown person near Chicago. The other was to a former doctor in Short Hills.

After I met with Cynthia Bullock, I saw her talking to a man in a car owned by that same doctor. The connection between

Cynthia Bullock and Wheeler is not direct; it goes through the ex-doctor, Derek Shaffer. But while it doesn't make them the three musketeers, it is nonetheless meaningful.

We know the least about two pieces of the puzzle, and that needs to change. One is the person that Wheeler called in Chicago the night that we grabbed him, stuffed him in the trunk, and brought him to the park.

Corey and Sam are out there trying to learn more, and nothing may come of it. Wheeler was from the Chicago area; that's where he was wanted for murder. It's possible he was calling a cousin, or an old high school buddy . . . maybe he needed money and was asking someone for it.

But it's also more than possible that the call was connected to what is going on; Wheeler's situation that night would have made it unlikely that he was making a casual call.

The other aspect of this that we have to get into is the Quantum Care Insurance company. They paid over $2 million to Cynthia Bullock, through Brisker and Moore Law. And an executive of theirs, Gerald Stoneham, was meeting with Brisker when they were both killed.

I would love to speak to Stoneham's wife, Emma, but Laurie called her and was rebuffed. Emma understandably said she had no interest in helping the people defending her husband's killer.

But she may know why Stoneham was in Brisker's office that day, and it could be crucial to our case, so I'm going to give it another shot.

I take a deep breath and get ready to dial her number. This is really important; I'm nervous and it reminds me of how I felt in high school when I was calling a girl for a date. I hope this call works out better than those did.

When she answers the phone, I say, "Mrs. Stoneham, my name is Andy Carpenter."

"I told that woman I did not want to speak with you."

"I know you did, and I understand why you feel that way. So let me put it to you directly. I don't believe that Nick Williams killed your husband, and I think that you may have information that could point to what really happened that day.

"Maybe I'm wrong; maybe Williams did it. Or maybe I'm right, and together we can find the killer. But there is no downside to your meeting with me; you can hear what I say and tell me to get lost. But there can be very significant upside; the person who did this cannot be allowed to go free, whether it is Williams or someone else."

She hasn't said a word in response; I'm hoping she hasn't already hung up.

"Fifteen minutes," I add. "Then, if it's what you want, I promise you will never hear from me again."

A long pause, then, "Okay."

We make a plan to meet tomorrow for coffee; it seems like all I do is suck down caffeine. But that's a small price to pay; Emma Stoneham has agreed to meet with me. Even Laurie couldn't pull that off.

I am Andy Carpenter, charmer of women.

'm just back from our morning walk; this time Ricky came with us, so I couldn't discuss the case with Tara.

But that's okay; we talked about the upcoming school year, and the Giants, and what the kids did on the trip. He told me that he wanted to spend his junior year of college abroad, probably in Spain or maybe Belgium. That can give me something else to dread.

As soon as we walk in, Laurie says, "Steven Loomis called. He wants you to call him at home." She hands me the number. "Who's Steven Loomis? The name sounds familiar."

"He's the new Jim Moore; I met with him the other day." When she looks at me strangely, I add, "He's the CEO of the law firm."

She smiles. "Right. And you're the CEO of your law firm."

"I know. It's lonely at the top, so we have a CEO support group. We get together once a month and talk about stock options and how much we like firing people."

"Are you going to call him?"

"Later, maybe. Much later."

"He made it sound important."

"I'm sure it is to him. But trust me, if he's calling, it's because he wants something from me, not because he's going to do something for me."

"You don't like him?"

"What tipped you off?"

"What did he do to offend you?" She smiles.

"He tried to hire me."

She laughs, "Oh, the horror!" Then she holds out the phone. "You sure you don't want to just call him?"

I shake my head. "He'll call back and I'll talk to him then."

The phone rings and I smile at the perfect timing. "Am I ever wrong?"

Laurie answers, since the phone is still in her hand, and then hands me the phone. As soon as I say "Hello," he says, "You sent Derek Shaffer a subpoena to testify at the trial."

"I already knew that."

"Why?"

"Because I'm calling him to testify at the trial. Did you play poker at the frat house the day they taught subpoenas in law school?"

"Derek Shaffer has nothing to do with your case."

"Then he can say that on the stand, and, boy, won't I be embarrassed."

"You'll be more than embarrassed."

"Is that a threat? And are you calling me as his attorney? Because usually only judges threaten me."

"It's a warning, Carpenter. I'm not some twenty-five-year-old prosecutor you can push around."

"Why do you care about Derek Shaffer?"

"He is a consultant to our firm."

"Out of all the doctors out there, why do you choose one who was thrown out of the profession for illegally writing digital prescriptions?"

"First of all, he is highly competent. Second, he was never convicted or even arrested. He voluntarily gave up his license because he wanted to move into a new area of the business. None of this concerns you."

"I would file that under 'it remains to be seen.'"

"Let me state this plainly, Carpenter. I do not want you fishing around desperately and bothering our people; they have been through enough. It is unacceptable."

"I am thoroughly intimidated. But since we're stating things plainly, it's my turn, and I'll do it as if I am talking to a twenty-five-year-old prosecutor. I don't give a shit what you want, or what you find acceptable."

Click.

And with that, Steven Loomis has joined a long list of people who have hung up on Andy Carpenter.

I hand Laurie back the phone. She is smiling, clearly amused at my conversation. "So you had a nice chat?"

"Yeah, nothing important, just two buddies shooting the breeze. We made plans to double-date real soon, maybe go bowling."

"That would be nice."

Moments later the phone rings again. Laurie looks at the caller ID and says, "Derek Shaffer." She hands me the phone.

"I am one popular lawyer," I say, before answering with my customary and clever "Hello."

"This is Derek Shaffer," the obviously angry voice says. "You sent me a goddamn subpoena."

"Everybody keeps telling me that."

"You will not get away with this."

"I already got away with it. You know how you can tell? You have the subpoena."

"I'm warning you, Carpenter."

"That's another thing everybody keeps doing. I have to say, I'm getting a little bored with it. So I will see you in court, asshole."

Click. This time I did the hanging up, and I have to admit it felt good. Maybe I should do it more often. I hand the phone to Laurie. "There will be six for bowling. We'll need two lanes."

"Seems like you struck a nerve."

"I know; I love when that happens. Try and get connected to whatever cop dealt with Shaffer's illegal-prescription case. I want to know the details."

"It's probably federal."

"Use your connections; you'll get to the right person."

"Will do."

Then it's back to real life and she asks me if I have time to walk Ricky to school before I go see Emma Stoneham, which I do. I've got a feeling that we are approaching the time when he won't allow a parent to walk him to school, even a parent as cool as me. This is a kid that has already hung out in Paris and Madrid.

As we approach the school, he sees some friends and runs toward them, yelling, "Bye, Dad," without looking back. Since I've been dismissed, I head back home, where my car awaits.

Emma Stoneham, to my relief, has chosen an old-fashioned diner in Leonia for our coffee date.

It's the kind of place with a hundred things on the menu, all designed to clog your arteries. I've got a feeling if you order a no-fizz latte here, they'll throw you out on your ass.

I sit at a table in the back and wait for Stoneham to arrive. She's ten minutes late and I'm starting to think I'm getting stood up; maybe the Carpenter phone charm has a shelf life.

Finally a woman comes in, looks around, and decides I'm the guy for her. She comes over. "Mr. Carpenter?"

"That's me. Thanks for coming."

She smiles sadly. "I almost chickened out."

We order coffee; I also get a piece of banana bread, but she doesn't want anything to eat.

"Please make this as painless as possible," she says.

"I will, and I'm of course sorry for your loss." I decide to get right to it. "Do you know why your husband was meeting with Charles Brisker?"

"I don't, but I know it was important, or at least Gerald thought it was."

"Why do you say that?"

"We were going away for two weeks; we had rented a house near Saratoga Springs. But Gerald delayed our going by a day when the meeting with Mr. Brisker came up." Then, "That delay is now going to last forever. . . . I'm sorry, I don't mean to be maudlin."

"I understand. But he didn't give any indication as to what was so important?"

"No. I know Mr. Brisker called him. They had gone to school together, but as far as I know hadn't seen each other in years. Maybe they emailed or texted; that I don't know."

She's calling him "Mr. Brisker," so she obviously had no close connection to him. It certainly supports her claim that her husband and Brisker had little interaction over the years.

"Gerald worked at Quantum Care Insurance?" I ask, already knowing the answer.

"Yes. For almost twenty years."

"What did he do there?"

"Well, that changed over time. At first he was in the claims department, an adjuster. Then he got promoted and was head of one of those groups. He was senior vice president."

"Specializing in medical malpractice?"

She seems surprised. "Yes."

I had taken a shot and it paid off. "But you don't know if his meeting with Mr. Brisker had anything to do with his work?"

"I do not. Can I ask a question now?"

"Of course."

"Why are we talking about this? Do you think Gerald was somehow a target? I thought it was just an evil, crazy person randomly shooting at people he worked with."

I decide to be honest. "I don't know if your husband was a target or was just in the wrong place at the wrong time. But I do know for certain that it was not a random crazy person, and that the police arrested the wrong man."

"He's your client, so of course you would say that."

"Actually I wouldn't. Will you be attending the trial?"

She shrugs. "I can't decide, just like I couldn't decide whether to come talk with you. Decisions are hard these days."

"I understand."

"People tell me that going to the trial would give me closure. They don't know what they are talking about."

"In my experience different people have different reactions and different results. But full closure is never on the table."

"You are very right about that."

We move to some small talk, or at least smaller than the subject of her husband's murder. She tells me that she's going to consider moving back to Ohio, where she's from, and where she has family.

Her world has been totally overturned and she's trying on the fly to prepare for the rest of her life. I gently tell her that I don't think it's the right time for her to make big decisions, but I'm not sure if she hears me.

I feel sorry for her and it gives me another reason to find out who put her in this situation and bring them to justice.

Corey and Sam have come back from Chicago to brief us on what they've learned.

I already understand from his two phone calls the last couple of days that Corey will never again travel with Sam.

Apparently Sam has driven him crazy with wanting to see what he called "real detective action." It got so bad that Corey asked me if I would represent him should he be forced to kill Sam. When I said I would not, he asked if I would recommend another lawyer.

They come to the house straight from the airport. Ricky is at a friend's, so Laurie and I are okay with the discussion taking place at the house and not the office. Marcus and Eddie Dowd are also here to listen to the update.

"The person Wheeler almost definitely called is Thomas Roden. Does that name mean anything to any of you?" Corey asks.

When no one responds positively, Corey says, "His name once came up in a case I was working on, but he wasn't a key player. In real life, he's a very key player."

There's no need to prompt Corey with questions to speed things along; he is not like Sam. When it comes to storytelling and a lot of other things, he is the anti-Sam.

"I used a connection to meet with Lieutenant Jeff Riker of Chicago PD, so that we could get information about Roden."

"We were both there," Sam says, prompting a withering look from Corey.

"We were both there," Corey agrees. "This is before we actually saw Roden. What we learned was later confirmed by the sense we got of him. By the way, he owns the restaurant in Highland Park that Russell Wheeler called that night.

"In terms of how he presents himself, he's a smallish guy, no more than five foot ten, maybe a hundred and fifty pounds. He's fifty-four years old and looks older; his hair is almost completely white. He considers himself a sophisticate and likes only the finer things; he probably has a wine cellar the size of Madison Square Garden. Sam got a photo of him that we can show you.

"He also professes to be a master chef; it's a hobby and a passion. One day a week he cooks for friends and associates at the restaurant; it's a set menu with no deviations. I've seen one of his typical menus; there's not a thing on it I would eat. This is not a hamburger-and-fries guy.

"Bottom line, you would not be afraid to run into him in an alley, dark or otherwise. But you'd be mistaken. First of all, he always has two bodyguards with him. I've seen them; they could be bookend tackles for the Giants.

"Secondly, he is as connected as they come . . . think Hyman Roth."

Marcus looks puzzled, so I explain, "Hyman Roth was a character in *The Godfather.*" Marcus nods his understanding, and Corey continues.

"The word is he can get anything done, including murder. He's rumored to have a piece of every illegal activity in Chicago and probably beyond, all without getting his manicured nails dirty.

"It makes perfect sense that if someone wanted Wheeler or

anyone else to do some seriously dirty work, they would turn to Roden. And they would pay very well for it. We followed him from the restaurant to his home; it sits on a hill looking down at the peasants below. *Palatial* would be a good way to describe it."

"So you saw him at the restaurant?" Laurie asks.

Corey nods. "We did. We did not approach him because it didn't seem as if it would accomplish anything, at least not yet. But based on how Lieutenant Riker talked about Roden, if we put him away, we'd get a ticker tape parade, and Riker would be the grand marshal.

"So that's basically it," Corey adds. "This is a guy who deserves to go down."

"How do we do that?" I ask. "And how do we do it fast? We're spinning our wheels trying to solve a puzzle, and while we're doing that, the trial is barreling down on us."

Nobody volunteers an answer to that, so I add, "We have to find a way to draw him out and to connect him more directly to the case. A phone call from Wheeler to his restaurant is not going to cut it."

"It's still all about the why," Laurie says. "Let's say that Roden supplied Wheeler and another guy to kidnap Nick and shoot up the law office. We're not talking about 1-800-DIAL A HIT MAN. Roden must be knee-deep in whatever this conspiracy is and why they were willing to kill all those people to maintain it."

"I think I may know the why," I say.

"Good," Laurie says. "Care to share it?"

"Not yet; when I'm more confident, I will. There's someone I want to talk to first."

"What do you want Marcus and me to do?"

"Good question. I'm not sure we've done enough to try and prove Nick was kidnapped and taken to the warehouse in Newton. Maybe you two can go out there and canvass the area. I know it's isolated, but they were there a lot. They brought Nick there, they took him out of there, and in the three days they kept visiting him, bringing him food. Someone could well have seen something and not realized anything was wrong."

"Good idea," Corey says. "Marcus?"

Marcus just nods, which for him qualifies as a ringing endorsement.

"What about me?" Sam asks.

"Glad you asked. I need a lot from you. I want to know if Cynthia Bullock held a life insurance policy on her husband."

"Okay."

"And I also want to know who Derek Shaffer and Roden called after Wheeler called them the night we grabbed him."

"I'm on it. Is that it?"

"Nope. I want to know all about Moore Law's cases in the last year as they relate to medical malpractice. And not just in Jersey, wherever they operate."

"How do you feel about rugelach?"

"I love it; that was going to be my next suggestion. Have you checked if they're available?"

Sam taught a computer night class at the YMHA and discovered that a group of Jewish seniors were incredible students. He's brought them in on a few of our cases when the workload became too great. We call them the Bubelah Brigade.

"Partially," he says. "Leon Goldberg and Morris Fishman have moved to Florida, but Eli and Hilda Mandelbaum would love to help."

"Excellent," I say, because they will be invaluable, and especially because Hilda makes unbelievably great rugelach. She is the Tara of rugelach bakers, and I don't say that lightly.

"I'll call Hilda now and tell her."

"Tell her my favorites are chocolate and raspberry."

didn't expect to hear from you again," Sally Montrose says when I tell her who's calling.

"I can be difficult to get rid of. I should have warned you."

"And I should warn you. I just got an email . . . in fact pretty much everybody got it . . . from Steven Loomis. He said no one is to talk to you."

"He's joking; we're buddies."

Montrose laughs. "I don't think so. Actually, I don't think I've ever heard Steven joke."

"So you won't talk to me?"

"Are you kidding? Of course I will. How else will I find out what Steven is so upset about? But I can't be seen with you; he is, after all, my boss. Can we do it on the phone?"

"I'd rather in person. There's something I want to show you. But the good news is I have experience with people not wanting to be seen with me."

"So how do we do this?"

I describe the area where I met with Karen Brisker near the back of the parking lot at the Bergen Town Center. We leave it that Montrose will pull up next to me and get in the passenger seat of my car. It's brilliant and foolproof; I should be in the CIA.

Twenty minutes later Montrose gets out of her car, looks around warily to make sure she's not being observed, then gets in my car. "Not sure why I care about Steven knowing about this; I still haven't even decided whether to return to work."

"What will you do if you don't?"

"You looking to hire an emotionally damaged lawyer?"

"Working with me is not the way to return to emotional health. Not doing well?"

"Depends who you ask. My therapist says I'm handling things really well; I beg to differ. What did you want to show me?"

I take a photo of Wheeler out of an envelope and hand it to Montrose. "Ever seen him before?"

She looks at it for at least fifteen seconds. "No, and I'm not sure I want to. Looks like a scary guy."

"Not anymore." Next I show the photo of Roden that Sam took in Highland Park. "What about him?"

She looks for a while. "I don't think so. Who are they?"

"Just people who came up in our investigation. Could be meaningless."

"That's a pretty evasive answer."

"Best I can do at the moment. Ever hear of Derek Shaffer?"

She nods. "Sure. He's a doctor we use as a consultant for medical malpractice cases. I've talked with him a bunch of times."

"He's not a doctor anymore. Why does the firm still use him?"

She shrugs. "That's above my pay grade."

"Was there anything unusual about the Bullock case?"

"Not really. I mean, it went very well, but the circumstances were such that it had to. The hospital screwed up big-time."

"And Charles Brisker handled it?"

She nods. "Yes . . . I mean, we all work on everything, but he was the primary."

"As a firm, do you monitor potential malpractice situations at hospitals and then approach the potential clients involved?"

She shakes her head. "No, they usually see our ads and come to us."

"Is that what happened in the Bullock case?"

"I believe so; I can't say I remember it for sure."

"Could Charles Brisker have been doing something unethical?"

"Unethical how?"

"As it relates to the Bullock case."

"I saw nothing like that," she says, maybe starting to get offended. "But . . ." She stops.

"What is it?"

"Nothing."

"You never know. What were you going to say?"

"Well . . . Charles seemed strange the last couple of days before the shooting. He was quieter than usual, maybe upset about something."

This matches what Karen Brisker, Charles's daughter, told me. She said her father was worried about something. "Do you know what he was upset about?"

"No, but he had a couple of closed-door meetings with Steven Loomis, which was unusual. But there should not have been a problem; business was never better."

"What about Steven Loomis? Any concerns about his ethics?"

"Not really. Steven is about making money, and he's very good at it. I'd really like you to tell me why you are asking all these questions. Do you think the firm is somehow doing something wrong?"

"I don't know. I'm just gathering all the information I can."

"This is making me a little uncomfortable. I mean, I have been a key part of the firm."

"It's not about you."

"Maybe Steven Loomis was right about you," she says, more with amusement than suspicion.

I smile. "Anything's possible."

It could be that we caught a much-needed break.

Laurie and I are on the way to the warehouse in northwest Jersey where Nick was held captive for those three days. Corey called about an hour ago and said that he and Marcus found someone we need to talk to.

I didn't bother asking what we would hear; if Corey and Marcus think it's important, then it's important. They said that they would be in a coffee shop in the small town about a mile from the warehouse, so that's where we go.

They're sitting at a table in the back with a guy who looks to be about seventy, though it could be that his gray hair and beard make him look older. At the moment he's chomping away on some fried chicken and talking with his mouth full. Corey and Marcus look like they would rather be anywhere else.

Corey sees us come in and his face shows his relief. He waves us over, even though he could probably have predicted we'd come to their table even without this extra invitation.

"Laurie, Andy, this is Ben Lacey. Ben, Laurie Collins and Andy Carpenter."

"Hey." Lacey puts down a fried chicken leg. "I'd better not shake hands; too greasy."

"No problem," I say.

"Ben, tell them what you told us."

"You mean about the warehouse?" He's still chewing his food as he talks.

"Yes, about the warehouse." Corey rolls his eyes. I can tell he's having trouble remaining patient with this guy. Lacey doesn't notice the eye roll, he's too busy chomping on the bread rolls that came with the chicken.

Marcus seems oblivious; he's eating a piece of pie, and he seems to have just cleared two plates of whatever food had been on there.

"Okay, well, I walk my dog every day, a couple of times a day, and we go down Conyers Street past where the warehouse is." Lacey pauses to take a drink of his soda. "That place has been empty for a long time.

"Anyway, I see this guy standing out front. A big guy, I mean, really big. He's just standing there, arms folded, almost like he's guarding the place. But I mean, who wants to guard an empty building, you know?"

I don't say anything, so Lacey repeats, "You know?"

"I know."

"Anyway, I stop to talk to the guy. I like to talk a lot, these guys will tell you that already," Lacey says, meaning Corey and Marcus. "But he doesn't answer me, so I ask him what's going on. So he tells me to get lost, and he takes a step towards me, like threatening, you know?"

"I know."

"The next day I saw him there again, but I kept my distance."

"I'll be back in a minute," I say, and go out to my car. I have the photo of Wheeler there, so I get it and bring it back.

I put it on the table in front of Lacey, and his face lights up. "That's the guy!"

"Are you sure?"

"Definitely. No question. Who is he?"

"Just someone that has come up in our investigation. Do you know what the dates were when you saw this guy?"

Lacey nods. "It's like I told them, I know the first day I saw him because I met my buddy here that day. We meet every Sunday for breakfast; we bring our dogs and sit outside. I told him about seeing this big guy in front of the warehouse."

"So?" I'm starting to fully understand Corey's impatience.

"But this was on Saturday, not Sunday, because we were celebrating."

"Celebrating what?"

"My birthday."

"The dates match," Corey says, trying to move this along.

"Ben, would you be willing to testify in court?" I ask. "All you'd have to do is say what you just told us." Whether he was willing or not, I'd force him to testify, but it's much better if he thinks he is doing so voluntarily.

"Around here?"

"No, in Paterson. We would put you up in a hotel. Are you married? You could bring your wife, and your dog."

"Hey, that would be great. Sure, I'd do that."

"Terrific. Do we have your address and phone number?"

"We do," Corey says.

"For now, I'd like you to come inside the warehouse with me, I want to show you something."

"Okay."

"Do you have a phone that can take pictures?"

"Sure."

I bring him inside the room where Nick was held and ask him to take a bunch of photos of it. When he's done, Corey looks at them and confirms that they're sufficient. With Lacey's permission, Corey emails them to me.

I tell Lacey not to discuss this with anyone, and he promises to only tell his wife. I don't want to scare him, but if the people we are dealing with learn about a witness favorable to us, the repercussions could be significant.

Laurie and I leave. Corey and Marcus are going to give Lacey a lift home, and I whisper to Corey that he should drive home the need for secrecy.

On the way back to Paterson, I say to Laurie, "We actually might have a shot at this. If we can get the jury to accept that Nick was kidnapped at his house that morning and held at the warehouse, then they can't at the same time say he was at Moore Law killing people."

"So we have Wheeler's phone at Nick's house, the neighbor who saw the strange car, and then Wheeler at the warehouse."

"Right, which might be fairly compelling. What we don't have is anyone to tell the story."

"What do you mean?"

"It's not enough to introduce this stuff; someone has to put it in context. Someone has to say that Nick was kidnapped and held, and the only person who can do that is Nick."

"Which means putting him on the stand."

"Exactly. And that invites a cross-examination disaster."

"But you'll do it?"

"If I have no other choice."

Sam asked me to meet him at his office. Well, not exactly his office . . .

Because Hilda and Eli Mandelbaum are helping him, there's not enough room to accommodate all of them, so they're working out of my office. Sam's office is the size of your average walk-in closet.

I'm looking forward to finding out what they've learned. The trial is bearing down on us, and we're not nearly ready. We just don't have enough weapons.

When I walk in, Hilda and Eli are hunched over computers in the conference room. They both stand and Hilda gives me a big hug, while Eli opts for a handshake. They have to be in their late eighties, but there is an energy about them much like mine, or much like mine when I was in high school.

"Wait until you see what I have for you." Hilda goes into my office and comes out with two boxes.

"Rugelach?"

She nods. "And something else. A chocolate babka."

"Hilda, you are amazing. Let's open up those suckers and get to it."

So I start with the rugelach and then have a piece of babka that is so delicious I make a decision in the moment: I am never going to go through another entire day for the rest of my life without babka. Based on this, if Laurie were to have a baby, I would push to name him or her Babka.

I'm feeling strongly about this.

Sam comes in from my office, sees what I'm doing, and asks, "Can you listen with your mouth full?"

I nod. "Mmmhmm."

"Good, because we've got a lot of stuff to go over. Hilda?"

"Me first?" she asks. "Cynthia Bullock cashed in an insurance policy when her husband died. It was through his work and was for ninety-five thousand dollars."

"Doesn't seem like very much," I say.

"It appears to have been a company perk, not something he took out on his own."

"Okay, what else?"

Eli takes over. "Derek Shaffer and Thomas Roden each made one phone call that night after Wheeler called them. Roden's was to a burner phone; there is no way to know who he spoke to."

"That's disappointing," I say. "And Shaffer?"

"Shaffer called Thomas Roden."

I smile. "That is whatever the word is that is the exact opposite of *disappointing*."

I'm going to have to process this, but it serves to tie things in a neat little package. Roden, Shaffer, and Wheeler were all connected, and somehow it all led to the shooting at the law firm.

If I had to speculate, and I am in a position where I do have to speculate, I would say that Wheeler told Shaffer and Roden about his encounter with us that night. The two men then discussed it, and the net result was that Roden ordered Wheeler silenced permanently.

That's my theory and I'm sticking to it.

"This is great stuff. What else do you have?"

Now it's Sam's turn. "Let's talk about medical malpractice. Just for some big-picture background, there are about twenty thousand settlements per year nationally, and the amounts total around five billion dollars a year."

"Wow. I went into the wrong area of the law."

"New Jersey is actually high up on the list. And the eleven states that Moore Law is in includes the top seven states on the malpractice list. They have averaged about a billion two per year. I have a list of the biggest cases they've handled, there are some beauties in there.

"Seventy percent of their income comes from medical malpractice cases. That percentage has increased every year; it's an industry unto itself. And ninety-five percent of these cases settle before trial."

Sam holds up a folder. "A lot of the details are in here, and we're still working on it."

"Great job, everyone," I say.

"You need anything else?" Sam asks.

"Besides more babka? Actually, yes. Take the four or five highest settlements the firm has gotten. Look at how much money they claim to have paid the plaintiffs."

"Claim?"

"Yes. Then if you can get into the plaintiffs' personal records, find out if the amount the firm paid is the amount they received."

"You think the two numbers will differ?"

"Not necessarily. It's just a hunch I have that I'd like answered one way or another. Something has to be shady with these transactions." I don't mention that the extra work I'm asking for will keep the rugelach and babka incoming trains rolling.

I stuff my face a little more and then call Eddie Dowd. I ask him to get Thomas Roden's name on our witness list, then secure a subpoena to compel his testimony.

"This is the Chicago guy?"

"Yes. Actually Highland Park."

"You want me to arrange someone out there to serve it on him?"

"No, I'm going to do it myself."

"Yourself?" Eddie's clearly concerned by the prospect.

"Myself. Well, I'll have Marcus with me."

W hy are you going to Chicago?" Laurie asks. "What are you hoping to accomplish?"

"Not an easy question to answer," I say. "I'm trying to shake things up. If someone gets angry enough, or worried enough, they might make a mistake. And we need someone to make a mistake."

"I understand that, which is why you're subpoenaing him. But why do you have to serve it yourself?"

"I'm not sure you've noticed this, but I can be very annoying at times. There are some people who find me irritating."

"Oh, I've noticed." Then, "But I'm worried about you. I can't go because of Ricky, but maybe Corey can go with you."

"Marcus will be more than sufficient. I'm not going to attack the guy; I'm just going to piss him off."

"We've seen what Roden will do when he's pissed off. Do not let Marcus out of your sight."

"Don't worry; I will protect Marcus at all costs."

"That's comforting."

I tell Marcus I'll meet him at the airport and he's waiting for me when I arrive. We fly first-class to O'Hare, which entitles us to a small bag of pretzels. Neither of us checks a bag, and we stay at the Airport Hilton, which actually has an entrance in the terminal. It's remarkably convenient.

Mercifully, Marcus agrees that room service will work for

dinner, so we each retire to our respective rooms. Dinner with Marcus, trying to make conversation, is less appealing than dealing with Roden.

In the morning I ask Marcus if he wants to go to Wrigley to take in a Cubs game; they're playing the Dodgers. He declines, saying that he wants to rent a car and drive out to Highland Park and get the lay of the land. I ask if he needs me with him, and he says he does not.

Corey has gotten us Roden's home address from Corey's cop connection out here, so we will have to decide if we want to serve him the subpoena at the restaurant or his home. Actually, Marcus will make that decision, and his trip out there today is to provide him the information he needs.

Since I basically have nothing to do today, I get a ticket to the Cubs game and head out to Wrigley. It's one of my favorite stadiums, not just because it's old and historic, but because watching a game there has a party atmosphere. I take a few photos of the place to impress Robby Divine.

Unfortunately, it's really hot today, and since I don't care who wins, I leave in the fifth inning. I don't even know who was going to sing "Take Me Out to the Ball Game."

There's still a couple of hours before I'm going to meet Marcus and hear the plan, so I spend the time thinking about the case.

I feel like I'm homing in on what the conspiracy is about, though I'm far from being certain. The problem is that no one is on trial for the conspiracy; Nick Williams is on trial for mass murder.

I wish I knew why the murders were committed. My assumption, and it is totally guesswork, is that Charles Brisker was the target, and the rest of the deaths were collateral damage meant to cover that.

But why kill Brisker? I can think of two possibilities. One

is that he became aware of the conspiracy and was considered a danger to reveal it. He could have been meeting with Gerald Stoneham not as an old school buddy, but as an insurance executive who was going to help Brisker expose the bad guys.

The other possibility is that Brisker was part of the conspiracy himself. Perhaps he wanted out and was acting in a way that his coconspirators felt risked exposure. So they eliminated him for self-preservation.

This theory is supported by Laura Schauble's having told me that settlement payouts were handled by Loomis and Brisker. If that is where the fraud was occurring, then surely Brisker either had to be involved or had to have knowledge of it. It also makes it increasingly likely that Loomis was in this up to his neck, which is why he has been so angry at my investigation.

But just demonstrating a conspiracy, even if we can show what it consists of, does not get us where we want to go. Moore Law could be as crooked as it gets, but that does not mean that Nick didn't walk in and start firing and killing.

Corrupt people are not immune from murder. Billy Joel may think that "only the good die young," but jurors and the judicial system would beg to differ.

Sam calls me with a stunning piece of news. As I requested, he has checked three of the four largest malpractice settlements, and then has gone into the personal financial records of the plaintiffs. In each case, they received substantially less than the listed settlement amounts, after deducting the Moore Law fees.

In Cynthia Bullock's case, she got three hundred thousand less than she was due, a significant sum by any standards. This tends to confirm a hunch of mine, that the firm was and possibly still is committing financial fraud.

While I have Sam on the phone, I pile yet another assignment onto the pile I have already given him. I ask him to thoroughly check into Brisker's finances; if he was involved in the conspiracy and was having second thoughts, his bank accounts should have built up quite nicely over the years.

Marcus returns from his reconnaissance mission and comes up to my room. He's been to the restaurant and learned that tonight is the night of the week that Roden serves as the chef there. Cooking is his passion and his conceit, and he makes a big deal out of this.

Marcus has called in a reservation for us for 9:00 P.M., which is the last hour at which the restaurant will accept them. His view is that we should serve the subpoena there.

We don't need to do it under cover of darkness; we're not interested in provoking violence, although I suspect Marcus would be fine with it.

I'm fine with the plan; there's even a chance that doing it in the restaurant will cause Roden some extra humiliation. I want to jar him into possibly making a mistake, and I also want to see his reaction.

Both of those can be accomplished by Marcus's plan, and the danger of getting myself killed or injured is considerably reduced. That is always a positive.

And if Roden really can cook, we might even get a decent dinner out of it.

oden's restaurant is small, only about ten tables. It's a comfortable place, not too fancy, with Sinatra music playing softly in the background.

All in all, a nice place to have a pleasant dinner, if it weren't owned by a well-connected thief and killer.

We park in the lot behind the restaurant since there are no spots on the street. When we enter, every table except two is occupied, though most of the patrons are well into their meal. It's a prix fixe meal, which seems a bit of a conceit since it's not a French restaurant. Why not just say *fixed price*?

But the bottom line is that there are no choices to be made; Roden is apparently not interested in cooking a lot of different things. Fortunately, Marcus and I both like what they're serving: a shrimp scampi appetizer, cherry-glazed pork chops, and tartuffe.

The food is surprisingly good. Roden would be an excellent candidate to work in the prison mess hall. He has come out a few times to chat with some of the customers and accept their praise for his talents.

He is as Corey described him, physically slight, gray hair, and a refined way about him. If I were a completely different person, I could kick his ass.

Two extremely large people sit at the small bar; I suspect they are the bodyguards that Corey described. I couldn't kick their ass with a bazooka.

By the time the waiter serves us dessert, only two tables are occupied besides ours. "Could you get the chef to come out here?" I ask. "We'd like to compliment him on a wonderful meal."

The waiter smiles. "I don't see why not. Thank you; glad you enjoyed it."

He goes into the kitchen, and about three or four minutes later Roden comes out and walks toward our table, smiling. "You wanted to talk to me?"

"Yes. Outstanding meal; I can barely push myself away from the table."

"Excellent. Always like to hear that."

"We even have a little gift for you. Marcus?"

Marcus takes an envelope from his pocket and hands it to Roden, who looks a bit unsure but takes it. As he does, I take a photo with my phone of the transaction.

"What is this?"

"A subpoena to testify at a trial in New Jersey. A man named Wheeler was involved, and as it turns out, Wheeler worked for you and you had him killed. Small world, isn't it?"

He shows no emotion, just says, "You're Carpenter?"

I smile. "It's nice to be recognized."

"Get out of my restaurant."

With that he drops the envelope on the table and walks back into the kitchen. He handled it all smoothly; this is not a guy that will be easily shaken.

I know he wants us out, but I still feel obligated to pay the check, and there is no way we are going to leave without first eating these tartuffes. So it is probably about fifteen minutes before we actually leave, though Roden has not come back out to rush us.

The envelope with the subpoena is still on the table, but I have photographic evidence that we served him, and the truth is, I doubt that I will call him to testify. I wanted to provoke something, but it remains to be seen whether I did.

We leave the restaurant and walk around to the back, on our way to our car. It's dark; if there are lights, they've been turned off.

Not a good sign.

"Your coming here was a significant mistake, Carpenter."

It's Roden's voice, another less than excellent sign. I can't tell where it's coming from, but that doesn't matter because suddenly on each side of us are the two bodyguards. That is the worst sign of all.

Roden suddenly appears ahead of us, and I say, "I'm an officer of the court and I served a lawful subpoena. You do not want to interfere with that in any way." I think my voice is shaking, but I know my legs are.

He smiles. "Oh, I don't?"

"No. Nor do you want to get your friends here hurt."

"We're not going to interfere, and you two are the only ones who are going to be hurt. We're going to make you sorry that you came here and make sure that you never bother me again. But don't worry, I am not going to have you killed . . . yet. Gentlemen?"

The gentlemen he is referring to are the two bodyguards who have been looming over us. He seems to be spurring them into action that will deter us from further annoying Roden.

Marcus hasn't moved, not an inch. He never does; I doubt that he has even blinked. When threatened like this, he becomes completely and totally still; I wouldn't be surprised if his hair and fingernails temporarily stop growing.

Nor has he said anything, which is also par for the course. I'm assuming and hoping he's awake because I'm sort of counting on him.

"Marcus, you want to handle this?" I ask, not expecting an answer, and I don't get one. I drop back a full step.

The two behemoths respond to Roden's direction in different ways. The one on the right moves forward toward Marcus, while the one on the left is nodding, as if agreeing with Roden that action time is here.

It's a mistake I have seen others make with Marcus. The only way to have any chance, and even then it's an extremely slim one, is to come at him from both sides at exactly the same time. And in this case, they may even think they are doing so. But I am talking Marcus time, which is measured in microseconds.

Watching Marcus spring into action is always stunning, even to me, and I'm used to it. I think it feels that way because he's always so silent, so still, just before it happens. When he does finally move, it seems to come from nowhere, but with a speed and power that is like a bomb going off.

Marcus's technique is to make sure his first move is decisive. He does not use a jab to set up a right cross; that's not his style. He wants to immobilize the opponent from the outset; and nothing is off-limits.

In this case, the guy who moved first gets to regret it first. He's significantly taller than Marcus, so Marcus rams an elbow into his throat. Doomed Guy number one makes a horrible gurgling noise as his larynx bears the brunt of the blow.

If he was a bass in his church choir, he'll be a tenor from here on in.

Doomed Guy number two doesn't even have time to take in what has happened to his partner. He pulls his right arm back to launch an attack, but there's an old adage, or at least there should be: never bring a conventional punch to a Marcus fight.

Marcus moves in and butts him in the head. More accurate, Marcus butts him *with* his head, but because of the height differential it hits Doomed Guy number two in the jaw. I'm not sure if it would be enough to make him go down, but the subsequent elbow to the side of the head ends all doubt.

He goes down next to Doomed Guy number one. The only difference is that he is out cold, while his colleague is still making gurgling noises.

I look at Roden, who is still just standing there, no doubt stunned at what he has just seen. "That go about as you expected?"

He doesn't say a word, just turns and walks back into the restaurant.

I mminent trials tend to motivate me to action, especially when I am operating at a disadvantage.

In this case, that disadvantage is significant, and I need to take chances to shake things up. And I need to do it now, since jury selection is tomorrow, which is a pretty good definition of *imminent*.

We're nowhere with either Thomas Roden in Chicago or ex-doctor Derek Shaffer in New Jersey. I've had Sam track Roden's calls after our meeting, but they didn't yield any special activity.

Laurie tells me that she met with a DEA agent who worked on Shaffer's illegal-digital-prescription case. "He was frustrated that they couldn't completely make it stick; according to him Shaffer had so many computer layers insulating him that a jury would have had a tough time getting through it. So they settled for him losing his license. The agent didn't say it explicitly, but my sense was he wanted to pursue it further but was prevented from doing so."

"Will he help us if we need anything down the road?"

"If it would put Shaffer away, I would think he'd be delighted."

But that does not change our situation. We know that both Roden and Shaffer are right in the middle of a conspiracy, but if we can't prove it or identify what the conspiracy is, then in real terms we know nothing.

We also know that Moore Law has been cheating some of its

clients, but it's hard to see what role Shaffer or Roden could play in that ongoing fraud.

But whatever is going on, Moore Law is at the center of it. Which brings me back to Steven Loomis. He overreacted to my subpoenaing Derek Shaffer, calling to berate me over it. My sense is that if anyone can be shaken into a mistake, it's Loomis.

So I call him again, and he takes the call. It surprises me a bit, but he probably is as anxious to hear what I know as I am to find out what he has been up to.

"What the hell do you want?" he asks, not the most pleasant conversation starter.

"I'm calling as a courtesy, lawyer to lawyer."

"Yeah, I can imagine."

"You're going to receive a subpoena to testify as a defense witness at the Nick Williams trial."

"Testify to what? I'll bury you and your case."

"Once again I'm intimidated; maybe this courtesy call wasn't such a good idea. But I know all about the Bullock settlement, and pretty soon the whole world, including the jury, will know about it as well."

"What about the Bullock settlement?"

"Nothing for you to worry about; you can call it a bookkeeping error. See you in court, Loomis."

I just fired the last bullet in my pretrial gun, and it probably missed the target. I'm just at a loss to know how to penetrate the conspiracy; the only potentially weak link was Wheeler, and he was eliminated.

I've had an idea what is going on for a while, but haven't verbalized it because my theory has holes that the average tractor trailer could drive through.

I think that Moore Law is somehow colluding with insurance companies to pay out larger settlements than the facts of the cases call for. Most likely they have people planted within those companies to shepherd their cases to the higher settlements.

Gerald Stoneham, the Quantum Care Insurance executive who was killed in Charles Brisker's office, may have been one of those planted individuals. He was in charge of a group that decided on settlements, so that put him in a perfect position.

Or maybe Brisker had discovered what was going on and was consulting with Stoneham on whether and how to go to the police with what they learned. I have no way of knowing if Brisker and Stoneham were good guys or bad guys.

In a perfect world, we could just follow the money, but this is a far too sophisticated world that we're dealing with. The firm is no doubt taking their fair share of the settlements, maybe inflated slightly but not criminally.

The key players, most likely Loomis, Shaffer, and Roden, are taking the money that the clients are not receiving. They're not buying CDs with it or putting it into their local bank at 3 percent interest. The money has been sent in untraceable wires to accounts we can't penetrate, to be taken out at their discretion.

So unfortunately, the holes I referred to cannot be filled with what I know to this point. For example, Cynthia Bullock, just based on the man in the car she was talking to after I met with her, seems on some level to be complicit in whatever is going on.

But how does that make sense? As Sam reported, she got less than she was supposed to in her settlement. It appears that the law firm ripped her off. That would make her a victim, albeit only a financial one. How does that fit with her being part of the plot?

Thomas Roden's prominence in all this doesn't quite compute either. By all accounts he can arrange anything, up to and very much including murder. He's probably responsible for bringing in Wheeler, and ultimately for the shootings at the law office.

So maybe he's the enforcer, designated to clean up if anything goes wrong in the conspiracy. But why is that so necessary? Is it a full-time job to be the vice president in charge of violence in a financial scam?

The deceased in these cases are medical malpractice victims. They haven't been murdered; that's not how hit men operate. In these cases, how would they even know who to murder? The plaintiffs aren't even Moore Law clients until after the malpractice has taken place. Who could predict that?

And the deaths are as a result of errors that the hospitals and doctors ultimately admit to. How could Roden play a part in that? Roden must be making a lot of money off of this, but does he bring enough to the party to justify it? I wouldn't think so, yet he must.

I also don't understand Derek Shaffer's prominence in all this. Is he just a medical consultant as Steven Loomis claims? Why would they need him? Is he somehow tied into the insurance companies? Does he have connections within hospitals to let him know who would be likely clients for Moore Law?

Settlements depend on a number of factors, not just the facts behind the malpractice. Obviously, the result is important: Did the patient die? If not, what about future pain and suffering?

Also important are age and earning capacity. It is this last area that I can see deception within the insurance company by an employee intent on getting a larger than normal settlement through. Is that what happened here?

One thing is for sure: money is at the center of whatever is happening. All of the players are not in it for the challenge, or the fun, or the excitement.

Neither am I.

You know there is a lot of media interest in a case when the gallery is packed for jury selection.

That's the situation today, with significant overflow outside. It took me ten minutes to navigate the media and onlookers in front of the courthouse; I'm going to have to arrange to use a side entrance.

Eddie Dowd is waiting for me when I arrive. As a former NY Giant tight end, he's more used to working his way through unruly crowds, though in his previous life they wore shoulder pads and helmets.

Richard Wallace and his team are already at the prosecution table, and he walks over, smiling, to shake hands. "Good luck, Andy."

"I'm going to pound you into the ground and stomp on your body."

He laughs. "Thanks for warning me. Dinner when all this is over? With Laurie and Sharon?"

"You got it."

Richard shakes Eddie's hand too and then goes back to the prosecution table. I'm going to have a tough time building up a hatred for that guy. I'll just have to mentally imagine he's part of something evil . . . like maybe he plays for the Philadelphia Eagles.

Nick is brought in, looking amazed by the size and energy of the crowd. Nick has essentially been in solitary all this time, so this must be something of a culture shock.

"Here we go," he says. "I can't believe how nervous I am."

"Just sit back and watch the show," I say. "And don't show any emotion, no matter what."

Judge Nestor Ramirez takes his seat behind the bench. Seventy-five people have been called as potential jurors, which is supposed to provide the twelve regulars and three alternates that we need.

In most cases, people come to jury duty armed with excuses and hoping to get out of it. This time will likely be different; in a case with this kind of notoriety, half the jury pool are probably planning to write a book about their experience if they get on the panel.

I'm going into this knowing that every single person we call, no matter what they say, is already familiar with the case. The coverage was just too overwhelming for it to be otherwise. I also believe that most come in assuming Nick is guilty; it's just a fact and human nature.

So the best I can do is go for the people I consider the most intelligent and open-minded. I'm going to have to change minds, and that's impossible if they're closed and unwilling to listen from the start.

The questioning begins and goes better than I expected. We go through fifty-two of the potential jurors and come up with the jury. I think it's a fairly good group, though obviously there is no way to know for sure.

One thing I've learned is that once the jury is chosen, I have to put the second-guessing behind me. It is what it is and they are what they are. My focus has to be on planting reasonable doubt in their hopefully impressionable minds.

As Nick put it . . . here we go.

Steven Loomis was worried, and the source of that worry was Andy Carpenter.

He did not know what Carpenter knew, or what he suspected, but that he was calling Derek Shaffer and Steven himself to testify was not a good sign.

His first call was to Sally Montrose, who had not yet come back to work after that nightmarish day.

"Monty, Andy Carpenter called me to testify at the trial. He said he's going to expose financial wrongdoing on the Bullock case."

"He asked me about that case a while ago."

Loomis was annoyed because he had specifically told his staff not to speak to Carpenter. "You spoke to him?"

"Before you sent out the word," she said, lying about the chronology.

"Are we vulnerable on that case? Could he know anything that we don't want him to know?"

"I wasn't that involved. It was more Charles; he was the primary on it. I don't know of anything. You might want to check with Shaffer."

"I will."

Loomis hung up and called Derek Shaffer and asked him whether they had anything to worry about.

"I can't imagine what," Shaffer said. "He's fishing."

"He's going to fish with me on the witness stand. I can't walk into that without being positive he doesn't know anything."

"Brisker would have been the guy to know the details. But I don't see how Carpenter could know anything. Let me look into it further."

"You do that, and I'll do the same. We have a lot riding on this; it cannot blow up in our face."

They hung up and Shaffer placed a call to Thomas Roden. "Looks like we have a potential problem."

"Carpenter?"

"How did you know?"

"He was here to see me. When that trial is over and the coverage dies down, Carpenter will be taken care of. It will give me great pleasure."

"Things might have to happen before that." Shaffer described the phone call from Loomis.

"I will take care of it."

L adies and gentlemen, you know why you are here" is how Richard Wallace begins his opening statement.

"You are very much aware of what happened in the Moore Law office on that fateful June day. Judge Ramirez has instructed you to avoid all media coverage of this case, but you had not been so instructed when the crime was committed. So unless you were vacationing on another planet, you are basically familiar with what happened.

"This was a horrible crime. I can't speak for Mr. Carpenter, but I'll bet he agrees with that statement. Six unarmed people were mercilessly and methodically gunned down.

"Where we differ is obvious. On behalf of the State of New Jersey, I am here to prove that the person who fired those shots is that man, Nicholas Williams. Mr. Carpenter will contend otherwise. That is what trials are for, and that is why you are here.

"You will decide which of us is correct.

"Rest assured that I am not going to ask you to take my word for it. When a man's life and liberty are at stake, our justice system demands proof, proof beyond a reasonable doubt. That is as it should be.

"So I will offer evidence which I believe will more than clear that burden. The evidence will be eyewitness, and forensic, and also circumstantial. I can confidently say that it will be conclusive and convincing. It will leave no reasonable doubt, none at all, that Mr. Williams committed this terrible crime.

"I'm not going to go on and on now. You will hear me talk plenty during the course of this trial, so I'm not going to subject you to any more than is necessary. I will let the evidence do the talking for me.

"So I thank you for your service. Your job is incredibly important, and I know you will do it honorably and well."

Richard sits down and I stand to give my opening. I cast a quick glance at Nick; he's trying to remain impassive, as per my instructions. But it's hard; he has just heard the government say that they want to put him in prison for the rest of his life.

It's Richard's approach to stand behind a lectern and speak, with notes that he occasionally and briefly refers to. It works for him.

My style is different; I have no notes, and I walk around the room as I talk. I don't know which is more effective with the jury, but it makes me more comfortable.

"As Mr. Wallace predicted, I completely agree with him: this is a horrible event we are dealing with. I've been a criminal defense attorney for a long time, and I've lived in Paterson my whole life, and I have never seen anything quite this awful.

"The person who committed this act should never see the light of day; he should be punished to the full extent of the law. There is no question about that.

"But Nick Williams is not that person.

"There is a conspiracy that has taken place in which millions of dollars were and are at stake. These murders were committed to protect that conspiracy, and Nick Williams was set up to take the fall.

"Yes, Mr. Wallace will present evidence to you that he will claim proves Mr. Williams's guilt. I can tell you now that it does not. It has been contrived and created, not by Mr. Wallace and his team, but by the conspirators.

"I will show you how it was done. That is my promise to you now, and it is a promise I will keep. And then I will ask you to right this wrong and give Nick Williams his life back.

"And I am confident you will. Thank you."

Some have speculated that Judge Ramirez might sequester the jury due to what will be intense media coverage. He's told Richard and me that he will not do so, at least not initially. But he's said that he will reserve the right to change that decision at any time.

For now, he forcefully instructs the jurors that they are not to watch any news at all, nor are they to discuss anything about the case with anyone, including their fellow jurors.

I've never believed that some jurors, in the privacy of their own home, won't turn on the television and see what is being said about the case they're on. But I can do nothing about it, and the coverage won't be any worse than it was during the time right after the murders, when Nick was missing.

Judge Ramirez announces that we will start court tomorrow morning with the initial witnesses. He dismisses the jury and Nick is taken back to the jail.

The opening statements went okay; the bad stuff starts tomorrow.

Richard's first witness is Sergeant Wilson Paradis.

Sergeant Paradis was one of a large group of cops that descended on the law firm after the shooting. Paradis was no doubt picked to be the one to testify because of his demeanor.

Paradis is in his late forties and has been a cop for twenty-three years. He has seen it all and knows exactly what he's doing, and that always comes across to the jury. He's a good witness, competent, measured, and unflappable.

Wallace leads him through his career, taking pains to list all his commendations. Wallace wants the jury to be aware that this guy knows what he's talking about, and I'm sure Wallace has accomplished that purpose.

"Sergeant, what made you and your fellow officers go to that office on that day?"

"There was a nine-one-one call made by a person on the inside; she reported a man with a gun."

"Had she said if anyone had been shot?"

"She wasn't sure. She was locked in her office."

Richard plays for the jury a portion of Sally Montrose's 911 call. She talks in a soft voice, obviously panicked.

"Please help me. I'm at the Moore Law office at 131 Market Street. A man with a gun is here; he pointed it at me and almost killed me. He may have already killed my friends. Please hurry."

"Are you now in a safe location?"

"No . . . I don't know. I'm locked in my office closet. Please hurry."

"Officers are on their way."

Richard turns off the tape and says, "Describe what happened when you arrived at the office."

"We went in from both the front and the back. We were obviously careful in case the shooter was still on the premises."

"Which door did you personally use?"

"The back. It was open when we got there."

"What did you find when you went inside?"

"A horrible scene. There were six murder victims in various areas around the offices. It was apparent that they died of gunshot wounds."

Richard shows photos of the scene, knowing full well that the jurors will be horrified by them. I can see on their faces that they are, and I'm sure these photos, and others like them, will make frequent appearances during the trial.

"Did you find any survivors?"

Paradis nods. "We found one person alive; the woman who made the call. Her name is Sally Montrose; and she was still locked in her office closet. Later on another survivor who had gotten away, Laura Schauble, returned to the scene."

"Was the shooter there when you arrived?"

"He was not."

"What happened then?"

"We called Homicide, secured the scene, and then searched the area, but did not find any sign of the perpetrator nor the murder weapon."

"Did you question Ms. Montrose?"

"Briefly; we left the full interrogation to Homicide."

Richard turns the witness over to me. There's little I can do with him. That's okay; he hasn't damaged Nick in any way. That is going to come soon enough.

"Sergeant, you said you briefly spoke to Ms. Montrose?"

"Yes."

"Did she tell you who the perpetrator was?"

"She did not. She was quite shaken up."

"When the other survivor, Ms. Schauble, returned, did she say who the perpetrator was?"

"She did not."

"Thank you. No further questions."

During the lunch break I see that Sam has left a message asking me to call him. When I do, he says, "It looks like your hunch was right."

"That happens every decade or so. What was it this time?"

"We checked into more of the largest malpractice settlements for Moore Law; I think we've checked eleven so far. Three of them were on the up-and-up; the firm paid the plaintiffs the amounts they were entitled to."

I'm not surprised by this; it's just further confirmation of what Sam already told me. "And the others?"

"Well, one was Bullock; I told you about that one. She got three hundred grand less than she was supposed to. The others were almost identical situations; in some cases the plaintiffs also got shorted three hundred grand, and in some others it was two fifty."

"Were they family members?"

"Yup. Mostly spouses. But here's the new piece: the firm paid out the full amount, but in two installments, part to the family, and part to a third party. The missing money, for example the three hundred grand in the Bullock case, was wired to an untraceable account. No way to know who received it, but I'm betting it wasn't Cynthia Bullock."

"I'm betting you're right; they are ripping these people off. Sam, I'm going back into trial; please email Laurie all the details about these cases. I'll call her and tell her to expect it."

I hang up and call Laurie. I describe to her what Sam told me, and what information he will be emailing her. "I need you to do something."

"What is it?"

"Contact some of the people that got ripped off and tell them what we've learned."

"Sounds like fun. Why am I doing this?"

"I want them to call Loomis and demand to know what happened; it's another way to put the pressure on him."

"I'll get on it as soon as I get the information from Sam. What about Bullock?"

"I'm going to go to her myself. I'm not sure where she stands in all this. On the one hand she was ripped off like the others, but on the other hand I saw her talking after we met with the guy in the car registered to Shaffer. On the surface it doesn't make sense, so I have to try to dig deeper. Part of that will be in seeing how she reacts when I give her this news."

Just before I go back to court I call Cynthia Bullock. She doesn't answer so I leave a message telling her that I need to speak with her again on a matter of great importance, and I ask her to call me back.

Whether she will is anyone's guess. I'll know at the end of the court day, because now I have to go back in and probably have to sit through what will be torturous testimony from Janet Carlson.

Richard does call Janet Carlson, the county medical examiner, as his next witness.

Janet is a good friend and strikingly beautiful. I can always imagine the jury's amazement that a woman who looks like this would choose an occupation in which she is dealing with dead bodies all day.

Janet's father was a medical examiner and she always says that's what she wanted to do long before she even applied to medical school. She claims to have an excellent "slab-side manner" and prefers patients that don't talk back to her.

Janet is another of those very professional witnesses that I hate so much. They just give the facts, without emotion or bias, which makes it extremely hard to challenge them. Jurors seem to hang on her every word, which is unusual. Often the testimony of medical examiners is dry and yawn inducing. Not in Janet's case.

Today I'm expecting her testimony to be horrible, and she doesn't disappoint. After Richard takes her through her credentials, he asks her to describe her actions on the day of the shooting.

"I was called to the scene at Moore Law. I was notified to expect multiple victims."

"Do you generally go to murder scenes?"

She shakes her head. "I do not. I have assistants that do most of the on-scene work. I focus on what needs to be done at the office, autopsies mostly."

"So this was unusual?"

"Yes. It reflected the circumstances. The crime and scene were both unusual."

He asked her to describe it, murder by murder. He shows photographs of what she's talking about and makes her talk about the terrible wounds inflicted in detail.

She does not go out of her way to sensationalize matters, but the descriptions, coupled with the photographs, have to leave the jury horrified.

I could have objected to what is overkill in describing overkill, but I've decided to wait and demonstrate it in cross-examination.

"Dr. Carlson, checking my watch, you've been on the stand for an hour and ten minutes."

She smiles. "It seems longer."

I return the smile. "It's almost over. Let me say a few sentences, and please tell me if that adequately conveys your entire testimony so far."

"Okay."

I nod. "Thank you . . . here goes. You went to the murder scene and saw six victims, in various offices, each killed by a single gunshot. Does that sum it up?"

"I would say so, yes."

"Is that what all the photographs showed as well?"

"Basically."

"But taking all that time, and showing all the photos, even though the jury has seen most of them before . . . does that make it more horrifying?"

"That's not for me to say."

I nod. "That's okay, it wasn't done for your benefit."

I expect Richard to object to my criticism of his technique, but he doesn't, so I go on.

"Dr. Carlson, did anything you see at the offices tell you anything about who committed this terrible crime?"

"No, but I'm not the one who has to figure that out."

"Thank you, no further questions."

Since it's Friday and getting late, Judge Ramirez sends the jury home and adjourns court until Monday. I wish he would adjourn it until February, but that's unlikely to happen.

I have a message on my cell phone from Laurie, who seems anxious to talk to me. She asks if I'm coming home directly after court and adds that if I'm not, I should call her. I am going directly home, so I don't call her back.

I place a call to Robby Divine and his assistant puts me right through to him. Robby always takes my call, bless his heart, even though I'm likely by far the poorest person who calls him.

"What the hell do you want at this hour?"

"It's four o'clock."

"Not here. It's midnight."

"Where are you?"

"Abu Dhabi. And it's hot as hell, and the Cubs lost again today, so I am in a bad mood. Which leads me to repeat, what the hell do you want?"

"I wanted to thank you for inviting me to the museum. I saw a carburetor that changed my life. It operated at the intersection of abstract expressionism and some kind of aesthetics. I forget which kind."

"You want to tell me what you really want, or should I hang up?"

"Do you know anyone high up at Quantum Care Insurance?"

"I know everyone high up everywhere."

"Can you get me in to talk to them?"

"When?"

"That's the problem. It needs to be this weekend, hopefully tomorrow. I'm back in court on Monday. It's pretty urgent."

"Okay if you talk to him on the phone? He's based in Des Moines."

"Of course."

"His name is Peter Irwin. I'll have someone email you his phone number. He'll be expecting your call."

"You're amazing," I say, because he is.

"Tell me something I don't know."

don't want to overstate this, but they were among the two strangest phone calls I've ever had," Laurie says.

"These were both people who got huge settlements in the medical malpractice cases?"

"Yes, and both of them, a man and a woman, were quite willing to talk with me. I made some excuse about representing a lawyer involved in the case, and they didn't question it."

"What did you ask them?"

"I started by asking how they came to be represented by Moore Law, and they both basically said the same thing. They saw the advertisements and called the number.

"When I asked if they were satisfied, they both said absolutely. They had nothing but praise for the firm. So then I dropped the bomb. I told them that I had information that they were short-changed, that the firm diverted part of their funds elsewhere."

"What did they say?"

"We're almost at the strange part. They asked how I knew that, and I said it was from a confidential but very reliable source. To further my credibility, I told them the exact amount they received and the date they received it. I also told them how much they were shortchanged. In both cases it amounted to over three hundred thousand dollars.

"And there was no reaction. No being upset at the possibility that this was true, no telling me I was wrong, no pressing me on who my source was, nothing. They just said that they trusted the firm and I had to be mistaken.

"I very definitely did not get the feeling that they would look further into it. And I know they did well in these settlements, but we are talking about a lot of money. And when I pushed it, and I mean gently pushed it, both of them seemed to get angry with me."

"Maybe they're happy with their settlements; they all made a lot of money as it is. Or maybe they don't want to revisit what was a painful experience."

Laurie shakes her head. "I don't think so; it's counter to human nature. You hear someone ripped you off for hundreds of thousands of dollars, even if you don't believe it straight out, you want to find out if it's true. You don't just let it go."

"So why are they just letting it go? You think they knew about it before you told them and are okay with it?"

"That's what it felt like. But I can't imagine why that would be. Why agree to terms like that?"

"Maybe they are unsophisticated and thought that's how things work."

"Maybe," she says, in a tone that conveys *No way.*

It feels like everything we think about in this case ends with *maybe*; I wouldn't mind a couple of *definitely*s at some point.

Tonight I'm going to go over the case documents again in the hope that something will jump out at me. I do it repeatedly during the case preparation and trial, but rarely does the jumping take place. The few times that it does makes it worthwhile.

First, though, we're going out to dinner as a normal family. We haven't done so in a while, and we need to focus on putting work aside and doing things like that. The documents can wait a couple of hours.

Ricky and Laurie love sushi, so we go to what they describe as a terrific sushi place in Teaneck. Since I only eat the few cooked things they have on the menu, like tempura and rock shrimp, it gives them a chance to mock me for what they see as my primitive, uncultured tastes.

I have to admit I don't get the whole sushi thing. Why would anyone eat something raw when they could just as easily have it cooked? Isn't that why ovens were invented in the first place?

When a waiter at a restaurant asks me how I like my steak, I say "medium" or "medium rare"; I would never dream of saying, "As is; just take it out of the refrigerator and hand it to me."

And they're always comparing sushi restaurants, whether one is better than the other. How is that possible? They are literally catching the fish, cutting it up, and putting it on the plate. Do different restaurants catch their fish in different places? Why wouldn't they all cast their lines in the place where the fish are somehow better?

The whole raw-fish thing is, at least to me, somewhat fishy.

But we have a good time; it's nice to laugh for a while and not have to think about murders.

Ricky talks about how things are going at school. He is on the debate team as well as the flag football team, so he's a hell of a lot more well-rounded than I ever was. He also seems to like schoolwork and even relishes learning, attributes that further distinguish him from his father.

When we get home, I check my emails, and sure enough, there is one from one of Robby Divine's assistants. It tells me to call Peter Irwin of Quantum Care at eleven tomorrow morning and gives me Irwin's cell phone number.

It's remarkable that in the middle of the night in Abu Dhabi Robby could make something like this happen, or even that he would want to. It makes me hope the Cubs can somehow get to the World Series again.

I go through the case documents for a couple of hours, but find no new revelations. I'm not surprised, but I'll keep trying.

Tomorrow is Saturday, so I won't be in court. That will automatically make it a good day.

That maniac called me from Abu Dhabi at two o'clock in the morning, his time," Peter Irwin says when I get him on the phone.

"And then he does five minutes on the Cubs. How they won't spend money on free agents, how they can't develop players on the farm, how they don't have a single pitcher who can throw ninety-five."

"He is somewhat obsessed."

"Why doesn't he buy the damn team?"

"I have told him he should. He says he wants to have someone to blame when they lose, other than himself."

"Robby doesn't lose often. Now, what can I do for you on this, a Saturday?"

"I know. Sorry to bother you, but there may be something going on at your company that you should know about, and that I need to know more about."

"What's that?"

"There was a case a while back, a malpractice case in Montclair, New Jersey. The plaintiff was one Cynthia Bullock; her husband, Gerald, died in Montclair General Hospital as a result of a drug foul-up. Your company was the insurer and you settled for more than two million dollars."

"Ouch. What do you want to know about it?"

"Actually, I'm not completely sure, but I have reason to believe there is an ongoing conspiracy about medical malpractice settlements, and the Bullock case keeps coming up. So, bottom line, I would hope you would look into it, top to bottom, and see if anything turns up as unusual from your end."

"You mean we paid out more than the situation called for? That maybe our people collaborated with the plaintiffs?"

"Both are possible, but I honestly don't know. What I'm asking is for you to go back and retroactively test the case against your normal procedures and see if anything comes up strange."

"This is disturbing."

"I'm aware. And if you find anything, it would not be an isolated incident, though your company would be one of a number that would be involved."

"I'll get back to you."

That went better than expected, so I decide to reward myself with a trip down to the Tara Foundation. Ricky hasn't been there since he got back from his trip, and he loves visiting there, so I take him, along with Tara and Hunter. They love it as well.

I may be the person who gets the most out of it. Seeing the dogs playing with each other and having fun, after having faced potential euthanasia in the shelter, refreshes me. Knowing that they will soon be in great homes is the icing on the cake.

I also get a great deal out of watching Ricky interact with the dogs. It's pure enjoyment, and I'm glad he is a dog lover. High up on the list of things I'd like to leave him when Marcus stops saving my life is this foundation.

I check in on Daisy, and Willie tells me that she's doing great. Dr. Dowling, our vet, says she should be ready to be adopted in days, and Willie has a home lined up for her. She is a truly beautiful golden.

He says that he's anxious for her to get out of confinement, that he knows what that feels like. I suspect he does; he served seven years in prison for a crime he did not commit.

Unfortunately, all good things must come to an end, and we head home. I will be spending the weekend endlessly obsessing about the trial and repeatedly reading the discovery, while football is on in the background.

Of course, Sunday night the Giants are playing the Cowboys, so that will take precedence over all else.

I'm surprised to get a return phone call from Cynthia Bullock. She is curious about the "matter of great importance" that I referred to, and she offers to meet me at the same Starbucks as last time. We're going to do it after court on Monday.

That's good news, except that it reminds me I'll be in court on Monday.

Richard's next witness is Jessica Espinoza. She was an admin in the Paterson office of Moore Law where the murders were committed, but was on vacation that week.

I'm sure he's using Espinoza just to give the jurors some basic information about the office. He doesn't want to use Sally Montrose or Laura Schauble for this purpose; he wants to save them for their key testimony later.

Espinoza can't be more than twenty-five and seems nervous about being here. "You worked at the Paterson office of Moore Law?" Richard asks.

"Yes, sir."

She talks softly and the judge asks her to speak louder so that the jury can hear her. "I will," she says, even more softly than before. "I will," she repeats, raising it a decibel or two.

In response to another question, she describes her role as an admin, which basically consists of doing whatever the lawyers and paralegals need.

"Did you know the defendant, Nick Williams?"

"I did. I do."

"What was his role at the company?"

"He did a lot of messenger work, bringing documents to the court, that kind of thing. And he was really handy; if the printer broke, or the copier, Nick could fix it."

"Do you know what his salary was?"

"No."

"He never talked about it?"

"Well, he told me that he asked for a raise and was turned down. That's all I know."

"Was he unhappy about it?"

I object, saying that the witness could not know how someone else was feeling, so Richard revises the question to ask if he ever expressed unhappiness about being turned down.

"Well, yes, he said he deserved it."

"Were you in the office the day of the shooting?"

"No, I was on vacation, thank God."

"Do you know if Mr. Williams was in that day?"

"I was told . . . Laura Schauble told me . . . that he wasn't."

He turns the witness over to me. Once again there is not much for me to get from cross, but I always like to accomplish something.

I know from her interview with the police how she felt about Nick, so I can make some headway with that.

"Ms. Espinoza, did you enjoy working with Nick Williams?"

"Oh, yes, he was always fun. He made me laugh a lot."

"Were you ever afraid of him?"

"Never."

"Ever see him violent or talk about violence?"

"Never."

"Ever see him show a temper?"

"No."

"Ever see him with a gun?"

"No."

"Did he ever talk about guns with you?"

"No, I don't remember him ever doing that."

"When you heard that the police were calling Mr. Williams a suspect, what went through your mind?"

"That it couldn't be true."

"Thank you."

Richard's next witness is the first one that can really damage us, and the potential for that damage is significant. It is Detective Ray Jameson. Jameson works for Pete in Homicide, and Pete thinks highly of him. He's one of the few homicide cops in Paterson that I have never cross-examined, so he's in for a treat. Of course Richard questions him first.

"Detective, were you the lead detective on this case?"

"Under Captain Stanton, yes."

"Were you at the murder scene?"

Jameson nods. "I was. The officers on the scene called us in, and I was the first from Homicide to arrive."

"And you questioned the witnesses that were there?"

"Yes."

"And as a result of that questioning, you had what you would call a person of interest?" Richard is being careful not to preempt Montrose's and Schauble's testimony; he doesn't want to dilute the effect they will have when they are on the stand.

"We had a suspect."

"Who was that?"

"The defendant, Nick Williams."

"You were confident of that?"

"Yes."

"What did you do next?"

"We got a warrant for his arrest, and a search warrant to search his premises."

"Did you execute those warrants?"

"Only one of them. Mr. Williams was not at his place of residence, and his whereabouts were unknown to us. We executed the search warrant."

"Did you find anything which furthered your investigation?"

Jameson shakes his head. "Not on the premises. But we subsequently found a handgun in a dumpster a few doors down from there."

"Was a forensics investigation done on it? And if so, what did it yield, if anything?"

"Yes, it was, and ballistics determined that it was the murder weapon. Fingerprint analysis showed a print belonging to Mr. Williams."

"Did that confirm your view that Mr. Williams should be arrested?"

Jameson nods. "Certainly."

"How long after that did you actually arrest Mr. Williams?"

"Three days. His whereabouts remained unknown for that time."

"Was it broadcast in the media that you were looking for him?"

"Very much so. You couldn't miss it."

Richard asks a few more questions to drive home the points he's already made, then it's my turn. Jameson has been a confident witness in his direct testimony, always turning to the jury to make sure they know he is communicating with them. It's effective, and therefore annoying.

"Detective, you said you executed a search warrant on Mr. Williams's home?"

"Yes."

"How quickly did you get the warrant?"

"We were there at six A.M. the morning after the murders."

"Did you find anything unusual?"

"What do you mean?"

"Were there any signs that he had left for a length of time? Any empty clothing drawers, things that appeared to be missing from closets?"

"Hard for me to know, since I don't know what was there in the first place."

"You wrote a report after the search, correct?"

He nods, and I hand him a copy of his report. "Is there anything on here that indicates you thought Mr. Williams might have been planning a lengthy departure? That based on what you saw he must have been on the run?"

Jameson frowns and hands the report back to me. He's getting annoyed, which just breaks my heart. "No."

"So is it fair to say that in terms of the executed search warrants, the only thing you found that you feel directly connects him to this crime was the gun in a nearby dumpster?"

"Yes. In terms of the executed search warrants."

"I had already said that. You don't need to repeat my words; try and use your own."

Jameson rolls his eyes in mock frustration; he's more thin-skinned than I expected. Richard objects that I'm badgering, Judge Ramirez sustains, and we move on.

"So we're going to talk about the gun, but first, what is your theory about how Mr. Williams got around that day and the few days after that?"

"We haven't identified that yet."

"Was his car in the garage when you executed the warrant?"

He nods. "Yes."

"So you think he drove to commit this crime in another car?"

"It's possible he took his car and returned it to the garage." I don't think Jameson likes where this is going. He's going to like it less when we get there.

"Are you aware that Mr. Williams happened to have his car serviced the day before the shootings?"

"I was not aware of that, but maybe he was planning to take

a drive. Maybe he wanted to make sure it wouldn't leave him stranded," Jameson says, more smugly than he should.

I introduce two defense exhibits that Eddie has gathered; he did a great job on this. I point out to Jameson that one is the record from the service appointment, showing that Nick's car had 71,342 miles on it.

"This is a notarized statement from retired judge Nathan Arkin. At the defense's request he examined Mr. Williams's car in the garage last week. You can see that he swears under oath that the odometer says seventy-one thousand three hundred and forty-five miles. That's a difference of three miles and reflects the distance from the service station to Mr. Williams's garage."

I'm sure that Judge Ramirez knows and respects Judge Arkin, but I add, "Judge Arkin is willing to testify to this if the court feels it's necessary."

"It is not necessary," Judge Ramirez says, and I turn back to Jameson.

"So if Mr. Williams didn't drive his car to the law offices that day, how did he get there? A cab? An Uber?"

"I can't say for sure." Jameson's getting worried.

"Did he pull up at the law office and say to the cabdriver, 'Wait in this alley for a few. I'm going to put my mask on and go kill six people'?"

"Perhaps he had an accomplice."

"Are you making this up as you go along?" I try to sound as disdainful as possible. "Have you found any evidence in your investigation of an accomplice?"

He doesn't answer, so I say, "Detective? Have you found evidence of an accomplice?"

"Not yet."

"Okay, let us know when you do. But for the moment, let's take any of the possibilities . . . a cab, an Uber, or an accomplice.

We can assume in this hypothetical that any one of those is correct.

"In your theory, Mr. Williams committed the murders and then left however he came, is that right? I mean, he didn't stop and grab a bus."

"Correct."

"So you think he said to whoever was driving, 'Before I run away for three days, stop by my house, I want to throw the murder weapon with my fingerprint on it near there'?"

"I don't know what was going through his mind."

"Do you know what's going through your mind?"

Richard objects and Judge Ramirez sternly tells me to tone it down. By this point, I suspect Jameson would be quite willing to strangle me and accept his punishment for doing so.

"Yes, Your Honor," I lie. "Detective, why would he possibly go back to his house to get rid of the murder weapon? And why wouldn't he wipe his print off of it? He clearly didn't go back to get any clothing; we've determined that. He wasn't returning his car there; we've determined that also."

"As I said, I don't know what was going through his mind."

"Right, I remember you said that. No further questions."

As I get back to the defense table, I can see that while Nick is trying not to show it, he's pleased with what I just accomplished.

Even though I am a cross-examination half-empty guy, I don't disagree. I made a lot of points that stumped Jameson and should make the jury take notice.

But I'm trying not to get too cocky because I know, and Nick should know, that worse days are coming.

park near the back of the mall lot. I want to be able to walk through all the other cars on the way to the Starbucks.

This way I can see if the guy who was last time waiting for Cynthia Bullock, or watching us, is here again. He was in a car registered to Derek Shaffer's company, which puts him pretty high on the suspicion scale.

I don't see anyone who could fit that bill; no one with a view of the Starbucks seems to be in their car. Of course, they could show up later.

Bullock is already sitting at an outdoor table, the same one we used last time. It's sort of becoming our special place. Fortunately, she already has her drink in front of her, meaning I don't have to go in and order something humiliating.

In fact, since I've been overdosing on coffee lately, I don't go in at all. Instead I just smile, say hello, and sit down across from her.

"We've got to stop meeting like this," I say, which is a joking way to get things started.

It wasn't a great joke, and Bullock clearly doesn't find it amusing. "It wasn't my idea. What is this matter of great importance?"

She obviously does not want to chitchat first, which is more than fine with me. "I have reason to believe . . . actually I know for a fact . . . that you received three hundred thousand dollars less in your settlement than you were due."

She looks more surprised than upset. "How is that possible?"

"I can't answer that; you were probably provided with incorrect information. But there's no question about it."

"What do you suggest I do?"

"That's up to you, but yours is not an isolated case, and it is all going to explode on that law firm."

"Does the firm know that this is your belief?"

"Yes, Steven Loomis claims to be looking into it." This is a lie, at least as far as I know. I want her to go to Loomis and increase the pressure on him. "But it's not a belief; it's a fact."

I've been counting on Loomis to make a mistake for a while now, and I'm running out of time for it to happen. This is a desperate Hail Mary to prompt that mistake, but it's all I have.

"Interesting," she says, not exactly advancing the conversation.

Now it's time to turn up the pressure on her. "Let me ask you a question. Last time we were here, after I left, you went over to a dark SUV and talked to a man through the window. Who was that?"

"How is that your business?" She is suddenly wary and probably worried.

"It isn't, and you don't have to tell me. But I'm in the information-gathering business, and I will find out."

She frowns as if annoyed, and she might well be. "I was walking towards my car. This man called me over; he was sitting in the driver's seat of the SUV. He said he saw me having coffee with you, and he wanted to know who you were."

"Why did he want to know?"

"He didn't say."

"Did you tell him who I was?"

She nods. "I did; he made me a little uncomfortable and I didn't want to start an argument. So I told him and then I left."

She's telling a smooth story; I don't know if she practiced it, but she told it well. I'm quite sure she's lying; there would be no reason for that man to have been following her, and if he was following me, then he knew damn well who I am.

Judges give an instruction that roughly says if a jury believes a witness is testifying falsely about one thing, then they can choose to disbelieve everything the witness says. The Latin phrase for it is *falsus in uno, falsus in omnibus.*

I'm going to apply that here, in English. If Cynthia Bullock is lying about the man in the car, then she's lying about not knowing she was shorted three hundred grand.

I just wish I could see past all the falsus stuff and figure out the truthus.

Richard calls Samantha Peterson to the stand.

Ms. Peterson is an accountant and an officer in the company that does payroll and human resources work for Moore Law.

Richard is calling her as a motive witness, even though he does not have to demonstrate motive. He knows that juries like to know why people they convict did what they are being convicted of.

"So you don't work for Moore Law, but you are an outside contractor for them? Is that correct?"

She nods. "Yes. We handle the payroll and much of the day-to-day office responsibilities. It's what many people would call HR. Obviously we do it in consultation with the executives there."

"Do you do that for them nationally?"

"Yes, though they only operate in eleven states. All key decisions come from the main office in Paterson, although that office is not open right now."

"Which executive was your primary contact, if you had one?"

"Mr. Brisker. Charles Brisker."

"Who have you been dealing with since Mr. Brisker's death?"

"Steven Loomis."

Richard puts into evidence an email that was sent to Ms. Peterson about possible raises for employees at the law firm and asks her if she is familiar with it. She confirms that she has seen it before.

"Who sent this to you?"

"Mr. Brisker."

"But the email came from Mr. Steven Loomis's email address. Why is that, and who is Mr. Loomis?"

"Mr. Loomis is the CEO of the firm, but Mr. Brisker sent this particular email from Mr. Loomis's address. That was quite common within the firm; people would send emails on behalf of others using their address. It was and is a very informal place."

Richard gets her to say that included in the email are raise requests, including one from Nick Williams. "Did you discuss this with anyone?"

"Yes, Mr. Brisker and I discussed all of these requests."

"Was Mr. Williams given his requested raise?"

"He was not."

"Why?"

"Mr. Brisker said that Mr. Williams hadn't been with the company long enough, that raises were not given before the end of the first year of employment."

"Did he say anything else about it?"

"He said that Mr. Williams would be unhappy about it."

"Thank you."

My first question on cross is "Ms. Peterson, you've been doing this kind of work for a long time?"

She nods. "Fourteen years."

"In that time, have you dealt with many people who were happy when they were turned down for a raise?"

She smiles. "No."

"So Mr. Brisker predicting that Mr. Williams would be unhappy didn't surprise you?"

"No, it didn't."

"Didn't set off alarm bells?"

"No."

"Did Mr. Brisker sound worried about Mr. Williams's reaction? Did he plan to have security present when he gave Mr. Williams the news?"

"No. He liked Mr. Williams and said he wished he could have granted the request, but it was company policy."

"You said you and your company handled HR issues for Moore Law?"

"Yes."

"Did Mr. Williams's name ever come up in any other context, beyond this raise request?"

"What do you mean?"

"Any complaints about his behavior. Any reports of threats? Violence?"

"No, Mr. Williams seemed to fit in well with the rest of the team."

"His job evaluations were good?"

"Yes. Quite good."

"Thank you."

Steven Loomis got the phone call from Cynthia Bullock a little after 1:00 P.M.

He had not gone to lunch; he was too busy dealing with the problems and stress that Andy Carpenter was presenting.

Not only was there the obvious legal jeopardy, but the business itself was facing an existential crisis. Whatever Carpenter came up with would be presented in the Williams trial, which meant it would receive intense media coverage.

The call that Loomis was about to take further fueled his concern. Bullock would not be calling him unless it was related to the Carpenter situation; Loomis had not spoken to her since her case was resolved.

His fears were soon realized. After minimal pleasantries, Bullock said, "I had a very alarming meeting with Andy Carpenter. He told me that I received hundreds of thousands of dollars less than I was due."

"He's been going around saying a lot of things."

"He said he has proof."

"He has nothing," Loomis said, though he suspected otherwise.

"I'm afraid I can't just take your word on that."

Loomis's initial reaction was anger. Who was she to be talking to him like that? But he knew that Bullock could pose a threat. "I'm sorry you feel that way; perhaps we should meet to talk about it."

"Depends on what you have to say."

"Understood. Can you come to my office this afternoon, say three o'clock?" As soon as he said that, he realized it was a mistake. She should not be seen at his office, not at this point. Carpenter could find out. "Actually, I'll come to you."

"I'm busy this afternoon. What about this evening? Maybe seven thirty at my house?"

"That should be fine."

She gave him her address and he promised to be there. That gave him the rest of the day to figure out the best damage control. One thing was for sure: it was going to cost the firm some money.

He had to make sure it was not going to be worse than that.

Laura Schauble is noticeably nervous as she takes the witness stand.

She is going to have to relive that terrible day in as public a setting as there can be, with the media breathlessly reporting her every word and action. The good news for her, though she probably doesn't realize it now, is that once this is over she can try to get on with the rest of her life.

Richard sees that she is anxious and smiles as he tells her gently not to be nervous. He wants to look like a good guy to the jury, and they will buy it because he actually is a good guy.

Under his direction, Schauble describes her role as a paralegal with Moore Law. He asks if she enjoys working there.

"I did. But I've decided not to go back. I need to move on. It might be the coward's way out, but . . ."

"I understand. Was it a close-knit group there?"

"Very much so. They were all my friends; we would spend time together when we weren't in the office."

"Was Nick Williams part of that group outside the office?"

"No, he wasn't." Then, "But I think everyone liked him. He just didn't choose to socialize, I guess."

Richard finally gets to the fateful day and asks her to describe the events.

"Well, it was a Friday, and usually we'd close early . . . Fridays in the summer. But Charles . . . Mr. Brisker . . . had sent an email asking us to stay late for an important meeting. He was in a meeting himself, so we were waiting for it to end."

"Do you know what your meeting was to be about?"

"No, we never found out."

"Where were you at the time of the shootings?"

"I was in an office next to Monty's . . . Sally Montrose . . . We were working on an important project together. So the door was open between the two offices."

"That was your regular office?"

"No. Since we were working so closely, Sally had the files moved in there and it made things easier."

"Then what happened that day?"

"I heard a couple of strange noises, so I started to walk towards the door to Sally's office. I stopped when I heard a voice say, 'Sorry, Monty.'

"I couldn't see all the way in, but I saw an arm extended with a gun."

"Was there anything distinctive about the arm?"

"Yes, it had a tattoo on it. It was a hook."

"Had you ever seen one like it before?"

She hesitates, as if not wanting to say it. "Yes, on Nick . . . Nick Williams . . . on his arm."

"And he called her 'Monty'?"

"Yes, that's what everyone called her. She's a lawyer, so she's on a higher level than paralegals like me, but like I said, everything was very informal."

"Did you notice anything else about the man with the gun?"

"I saw one of his feet; it was forward ahead of the other one. He was wearing a sneaker with red and yellow stripes."

"Had you seen them before?"

"Well, Nick always wore sneakers just like that."

"What did you do after you saw and heard this man?"

"I ran. I guess I just panicked and I ran out of the office through the back door. It was open. Then I ran down the street."

"So you never saw anyone come out?"

"No."

Richard turns her over to me. I certainly don't want to badger her, both because I like her and, more important, I'm sure the jury likes her as well. But I need to make some points.

"Ms. Schauble, please describe your relationship with Nick Williams."

"Well, I always thought we were friends. He was funny and made me laugh."

"Would you say he was well-liked in the office?"

"Yes, for sure."

"Ms. Schauble, you say that everyone called Ms. Montrose by her nickname, Monty?"

"Yes."

"Was that limited to people in the office? What about her friends outside of work?"

"I think everyone called her that. I was once at a party she threw, and I'm pretty sure her friends used that name."

"If you talked to people about her, people that didn't know her, might you have used the nickname? Or would you have referred to her as Sally Montrose?"

"Probably I'd say Monty. I'm not sure."

"So this was not some secret name, some special code name that people in an exclusive club used?"

Laura smiles. "No. We were not in a secret club."

"You said you heard the killer say, 'Sorry, Monty.' Did you recognize his voice?"

"Not really. But I was really nervous."

"Let's talk about the tattoo." I introduce two photos of an

arm, both with tattoos in the shape of a flower, as well as a statement describing them.

"Have you ever seen these photos before?"

"No."

"I can tell you that one of them is a permanent tattoo and one is temporary. The temporary one was applied and can be removed in minutes." I had filed documentation with the court that states under oath which is which. "Can you tell me which is the permanent one?"

She looks at them for a while. "No, they look the same to me."

"So based on that, would you say it's possible that the tattoo you saw on the killer's arm was a temporary one?"

"I suppose."

"Thank you, Ms. Schauble."

Cynthia Bullock saw Steven Loomis's car pull up in front of her house.

With the huge malpractice settlement she got after the death of her husband, Gerald, she had moved into an exclusive neighborhood in Montclair. Each house on the street had a large piece of property, so no neighbors were close by.

Those neighbors had long tried to protect the ambience of the neighborhood by not having streetlights, so the area at night was obviously always quite dark. Bullock did not have the lights on in front of her house, so the headlights from Loomis's car were glaring.

He turned his car off and she heard him slam the door. She could no longer see him through the front window, though she continued to look.

It didn't matter; she knew what was going to unfold. He was going to approach the front door; that was probably happening at that moment.

Two men were going to come out of the shadows and grab him. They would overpower him, and if he resisted, they would likely knock him into unconsciousness. They might do that even if he was passive.

Bullock thought she heard noises, and an aborted yell of protest, so that part of the operation had already been accomplished.

The men would then put Loomis into the trunk of their car,

which was in her driveway. One of them would then drive away. The other man would take Loomis's car keys and leave in his car. The car would then be disposed of; she did not know where.

Soon, Steven Loomis would be killed; she was certain of that. He might be dead already. She had no idea if the body would ever be found, but she doubted it.

She would wait about a half hour and then place a call to Loomis. She would get his voice mail and leave a message questioning where he was, and asking why he did not show up for their meeting.

She was not proud of her role in all of this, but was not conscience-stricken either. It was all part of a deal she'd made a long time ago, a deal from which there was no turning back.

Cynthia Bullock was unaware of one issue while she was visualizing what was happening to Steven Loomis.

The issue went by the name of Marcus Clark.

Marcus was following Loomis and pulled up down the street from Bullock's house, then approached by foot. There was just enough moonlight for Marcus to see the two men that were waiting for Loomis not far from the front door, and to see them grab him.

Loomis started to yell something but stopped when one of the men viciously punched him in the head. He slumped to the ground, and the other man reached down to pick him up.

That's when Marcus arrived.

Since one of the men was leaning over and grabbing Loomis, Marcus decided to deal with the other man first. He did so with a punch to the gut, causing the man to lurch down into a Marcus Clark elbow. He was unconscious long before he hit the ground.

Stunned by what had just taken place, the other man let go of Loomis and turned to see what was happening. Turning was not the smart move; he should have been running.

Since Marcus had seen the man with both of his hands on Loomis, he knew he was not holding a gun. That allowed Marcus to take his time. He threw a straight left jab into the man's nose, not so much fracturing it as squashing it. Next came a right cross, which sent the man to the ground, or technically on top of his unconscious partner.

Loomis, groggy himself, looked up and asked the obvious question: "What the hell is going on?"

Laurie and I arrive at Cynthia Bullock's house fifteen minutes after receiving Marcus's call.

Marcus is about twenty feet in front of the house with Steven Loomis, who looks shaken up and seems to have dried blood on the side of his face.

A two-man, unconscious pile is lying on the ground near them. One of the men seems larger than the other. He is the one on top, and he almost obscures the smaller guy underneath him. They could be dead; I have no idea.

Marcus had told Laurie on the phone essentially what happened, that he had been following Loomis and two guys jumped him when he approached Bullock's house. Marcus intervened, and the result of that intervention is the thug pile on the ground.

In the front of the house, I can see Cynthia Bullock peering out at us, pulling aside the drapes to sneak a glimpse at the edge of the window. I have no idea if she knows what's going on, or whether she had a role in it. My focus is on Loomis.

"He saved my life," Loomis says, meaning Marcus.

"He's good at that," I say. "Who are these guys?"

"I have no idea."

"What are you doing here?"

"I came to talk to Mrs. Bullock about her case."

"What about it?"

"You know what about it. She received less money than she was entitled to."

"So why were these guys after you?"

"I don't know," Loomis says.

"Bullshit."

Suddenly the street is lit up as a bunch of patrol cars, colorful lights flashing, pull up to the house. Cynthia Bullock obviously called them.

I need to talk quickly. "You need to talk to me, Steven. You owe us that, you need to do the right thing, and you can save yourself in the process."

He looks at me and nods. "Call me tomorrow."

The police reach us, and fortunately Laurie knows the detective in charge. She tells them what happened from our perspective and we leave the scene, after confirming with Marcus that he is okay and can handle things from here.

One of the cops shines his flashlight on the two men on the ground. I don't say anything, but it hits me immediately. One of the men is face up, and I am positive he is the guy that was watching me at the Starbucks when I met with Cynthia Bullock.

I'm anxious to find out who the two assailants are, and very much looking forward to talking to Loomis tomorrow, if he doesn't change his mind.

On the way home Laurie asks, "Why would they have wanted to kill Loomis?"

"We don't know that they were going to kill him; maybe they were going to stash him in a warehouse somewhere like they did to Nick. But killing him seems the most likely. As to the why, I wish I knew."

"What's your best guess?"

"That Loomis and Brisker were in on the conspiracy, and

their partners were afraid they were going to talk and bring the whole thing down."

"There's a problem with that. Sam called earlier and said that he could not find anything unusual in Brisker's finances."

"Doesn't matter; these guys would have been good at hiding their money."

She shakes her head. "It still doesn't make sense. If the conspiracy is the withholding of money from their clients . . . not paying them what they are due . . . then Loomis and Brisker were essential to it. Killing them would put an end to it."

"That's true. And Loomis and Brisker were also the ones that would take the fall if it was discovered. Why would they deliberately sabotage it by going to the police or doing something else? Why turn in their colleagues if it would only cause them to go down?"

"I'll go you one better. Why would they need colleagues at all? This was simple fraud, conducted within their company. Why the outside doctor, Shaffer? Why the need for a connected guy in Chicago?"

"All good questions, none of which I can answer," I say. "Maybe the shootings had nothing to do with this conspiracy; is that possible? Maybe they're unconnected; maybe there is something else entirely going on that I'm just missing."

"We don't have much time to figure it out."

"You mean because of the trial? That's not really true, and that's the worst part of it. At this point all of this has nothing to do with the trial, at least not in real life.

"Suppose we could prove, I mean prove right now, that there was fraud going on. How does that get Nick acquitted? A mass murder in a company that happens to be committing financial fraud is just as bad as a mass murder anywhere else. We don't have to just show fraud; we have to show that it led to the shootings."

She smiles. "The other reason we don't have a lot of time is that Marcus is getting frustrated. A frustrated Marcus is dangerous."

"Hopefully he got to release some of that pressure tonight. Why the hell was he following Loomis?"

"Because he had nothing better to do, and because Loomis seems like the most likely suspect. I gave him the okay to free-lance because I had no specific assignment for him. He wanted to know who Loomis was meeting with."

"Turned out lucky for Loomis," I say. "And not so lucky for those two guys."

"If whoever sent those guys was afraid that Loomis will rat them out, I would think he'd have more reason to do so now."

"Maybe. But I can't say I'm confident about it."

"Where do you think Cynthia Bullock stands in all this?"

"Up to her neck. Those guys didn't follow Loomis; they were waiting for him. It's a good bet that she told them he was coming."

"She wasn't looking to have him killed because the firm paid her less than she was owed. It has to be something more than that."

"Yes, it does."

Sally Montrose is Richard's star witness, though she doesn't look anxious to make her debut as a celebrity.

Like Laura Schauble, she looks like she'd rather be anywhere else than here. For them, this case is the nightmare that keeps on giving.

I'm not looking forward to this either. The day already started on a bad note; Peter Irwin of Quantum Care called this morning to say that he did a thorough internal check and there was nothing unusual about the Bullock settlement. If anything, he said, the prevailing view was that they might have gotten off a little cheaper than expected.

That effectively kills off one of the possible theories, that the conspirators had someone within the insurance companies authorizing higher settlement amounts than the cases called for. All that leaves is the plaintiffs not getting all the money that was coming to them; we already have evidence of that.

Montrose explains her role at Moore Law; she's a lawyer who worked for Brisker, and ultimately for Loomis. She worked on all kinds of cases with many clients; it was a collaborative workplace where everybody pitched in where needed.

"And you knew Nick Williams?" Richard asks.

"Yes, of course. Nick was around every day."

"You considered him a friend?"

She thinks for a moment. "Depends on your definition, I guess.

We were certainly friendly in the office; I liked him and thought we had a good relationship. But we didn't hang out socially or anything like that. I guess you could say we were workplace friends."

"And he would have known the layout of the office? For example, where each person's office was?"

"Certainly. Nick . . . Mr. Williams . . . was there every day."

"Except the day of the shooting. He did not come in that day?"

"He did not."

"Had he called or contacted anyone to explain why he was not there?"

"Not that I know of. It was very unusual; he was always conscientious."

Richard asks her to describe what happened that afternoon, and she takes a deep breath, preparing herself for the ordeal.

"I was in my office, working at my desk. Laura Schauble was in the office next to mine, and the door was open between us. I didn't hear anything unusual, and then suddenly I looked up and there was a man there, with a black ski mask on, pointing a gun at me."

Her voice is shaking a bit as she adds, "It is something I will certainly never forget."

"What happened next?"

"The man with the gun said, 'Sorry, Monty,' and he raised the gun to fire. It was pointed at my heart. Then he must have heard a noise; I found out later it was Laura running away. He turned and quickly left my office, probably to see what the noise was.

"I was stunned and sat there for a few seconds. Then I got up and locked my office door and went into my closet. I called nine-one-one and stayed there until the police showed up. At any moment I thought the man would come back and kill me."

"But he did not come back?"

"I didn't hear him if he did. He certainly didn't try to get into the closet . . . thank God."

"How long did it take for the police to get there?"

"Later on I was told it was six minutes; it seemed like a lot longer."

Richard asks her if she noticed anything about the man that would help her identify him, and she explains about the hook tattoo on his arm.

"Mr. Williams has a tattoo just like that, in the same place."

"Anything else?"

"He was wearing sneakers; they had red and yellow stripes on them. Nick wears them all the time. And he stood and walked like Nick does, very upright."

"Would Nick have known your nickname was Monty?"

"Definitely. That's what he called me."

"Did you recognize the man's voice?"

She nods. "It sounded like Nick."

"Do you have any doubt that it was Nick Williams who was pointing the gun at you?"

She pauses for a moment and steals a quick glance at Nick at the defense table. Then, "I believe it was Nick."

In my cross-examination, I start off with similar questions to the ones I asked Laura Schauble.

"Ms. Montrose, do only people in the office know you as Monty?"

"No, my friends outside the office do also. Everybody calls me that."

"So it's not a special name that only you and Mr. Williams knew about?"

"Definitely not."

"You said the man was wearing sneakers with red and yellow stripes, the kind Mr. Williams wears."

"Yes."

I show her a photo of the sneakers. "Are these the sneakers you are talking about?"

"Yes."

"Would it surprise you to know that more than one hundred and ten thousand pairs of these shoes were sold last year, and twelve thousand seven hundred and forty were sold in the New York metropolitan area?"

"I wouldn't know either way."

I turn to the tattoo and show her the same photographs I showed Laura Schauble. Montrose also cannot tell which is the permanent hook tattoo and which is the temporary one.

"You said the shooter was wearing a mask. Was he wearing a short-sleeve shirt?"

"Yes."

"Which enabled you to see the tattoo?"

"Yes."

"Wouldn't he have known you could identify it?"

She thinks for a moment. "Yes, he would have known that. But I think he was planning to kill everyone, so no one could identify him."

"So why wear a mask?"

"That's a good question . . . I don't know."

"Ms. Montrose, did you ever have any concern about Mr. Williams? That he might do something violent?"

"Never."

"Thank you."

Judge Ramirez asks Richard to call his next witness, but Richard tells him that the prosecution rests their case. The judge says that we will resume tomorrow with the defense case.

It's our turn.

I'm starting to get a complex.

Steven Loomis, like a few other people involved with this case, does not want to be seen with me. Of course in this instance, since it's apparent that people are trying to kill him, I'm fine with that.

But Loomis is standing by his promise to talk to me; he just doesn't want to do it at his office or in a public place. I suggested my office, and he agreed, though somewhat reluctantly.

I've come here right after court and done some work while waiting for Loomis to arrive. Finally I hear footsteps coming up the steps, so I look out my office door and see him making his way up.

He sees me. "This is really your office?"

"Yeah. It's a little fancy and expensive for my taste, but I thought I'd indulge just this once. And it impresses the hell out of my clients."

He reaches the office, looks in. "If I hired you, I'd give you a cubicle nicer than this. It's a shithole."

"It's an acquired taste. You want something to drink? I've got Diet Coke and water."

He asks for a water and I go to get it. When I come back, he says, "I never got a chance to thank your guy for saving my life."

"Marcus is his own guy. Do we know the identity of the two men who grabbed you?"

He nods. "One is from Chicago, one is local. They seem to be hit men. Hit men." He says it twice as if trying to get his mind around it.

"Why you?"

"I have no idea."

"Bullshit."

"I swear. I have no idea."

"Let's start with the fact that you were paying plaintiffs less than they should have gotten. Cynthia Bullock for one."

He nods. "I'm looking into that, but I'm afraid you are right. I didn't know about it, but I am going to make good on it."

"Then who did it?"

"Charles Brisker."

"Throwing the dead guy under the bus."

"I'm telling you the truth; he dealt with the banks on those matters."

"There's more to it than just the underpayments. Six people are dead; you would have been number seven. Your partners are cleaning up loose ends, of which you are one. Brisker was another."

"Whoever they are, they are not my partners."

"Did I mention that was bullshit?"

"You did, but you're wrong."

The distress on his face is evident and seems to border on panic. It's just a sign that I have to increase the pressure and hope he caves.

"You were a part of it, and now you have been protecting your coconspirators, who returned the favor by trying to kill you. They are murderers, which makes you a murderer, whether or not you pulled the trigger."

"No, I swear."

"Why did you come here? To tell me what I already know, that you cheated your clients?"

"I told you I would talk to you, so I came here to fulfill my promise."

"I'm going to reveal the fraud on the witness stand. I'm going to take you apart, and the media will cover every word of it."

He nods. "It will destroy our company."

"That's terribly upsetting, but I'll get over it. Now get the hell out of here."

This may be the toughest decision I have ever had to face in presenting a case.

It concerns my client's testifying in his own defense, but it's not about whether he will testify. I have already made that decision: Nick Williams is going to take the stand.

Nick is the only one who can testify to what happened to him on the morning of the shooting and in the three days thereafter. There is simply no other way to get it in.

But the key question is when he should relate it. I have corroborating evidence, but it would make little sense to the jury if my witnesses testify about what they know without Nick having set it up. The jury would have no idea what they are talking about.

On the other hand, Nick would have more credibility if he follows those witnesses; he wouldn't be telling a story with no corroboration.

So if he goes first, he risks not being credible and would face a stiffer cross-examination by Richard. If he goes last, we risk confusing the jury with witness testimony preceding him that has no context.

"Tara, what do you think I should do?" I ask, midway through our walk.

She turns toward me and gives her cute head tilt; no one tilts their head as cute as Tara. But she's giving me a message; she's saying, *What are you asking me for? I told you not to take the damn case.*

I can't say that I'm thrilled with her attitude, but Tara doesn't beat around the bush. I can't dump this off on anyone else. But I can't decide what to do, which is an unacceptable situation when a decision is absolutely necessary.

So I make one.

Nick will testify at the end, to wrap up the defense case. If he goes first, and Richard takes him apart, then the damage will have been done and the witnesses to follow will have far less impact.

If he goes last, then the jury might be confused by the earlier witnesses, but at least they'll be engaged in wondering where all this will lead. Nick will have more credibility and more impact.

Unless I'm wrong.

My first witness is Sergeant Tina Winston.

She works in the cybercrime division of the New Jersey State Police. Sam says he knows her from some workshop they both attended a while back, and he liked her and said she's smart.

That is why we chose her, but I doubt that she is happy about it, especially now. Cops have a general and understandable aversion to testifying for the defense. She agreed to do it outside of her job, and we are paying her for her time and expertise.

Included in the discovery had been the number of the cell phone that Russell Wheeler had with him when he was murdered at the motel. We had already known the number, but couldn't say so because Sam had gotten it by illegally breaking into the phone company's computer.

So we subpoenaed records that Sam had already obtained, but which we can now use as evidence. It's the only way we could do it.

I take Sergeant Winston through her credentials; she comes off as authoritative and impressive. Plus, she calls me "sir."

I introduce the phone records and ask her what they represent.

"Almost every cell phone has a GPS device in it which records where the phone is at all times. These are the records for a particular phone during a particular time frame."

"Thank you. I refer you to the morning of June twenty-eighth between seven and eight o'clock. Do you see those records?"

"I do, sir."

I get her to say that the phone spent forty-five minutes at Nick Williams's home address in Clifton, after which it went to the warehouse location in northwest Jersey.

"How long did it spend there?"

"Almost an hour, though it returned there repeatedly over the next few days. Altogether it was there for close to seven hours."

"Whose name is this phone listed in?"

"A Ms. Elaine Attwood, sir."

"Did I ask you to locate Ms. Attwood?"

"You did, but I determined that she does not exist. It is a fake name."

"Where was this phone found by the Paterson police?"

"In a motel in Garfield; in the possession of a Mr. Russell Wheeler."

"Did you make inquiries as to who Mr. Wheeler is?"

"Yes, sir. At the time there was a warrant out for his arrest on a murder charge in Chicago."

"Where is Russell Wheeler today, if you know?"

"He's deceased. He was murdered in that motel room in Garfield, a few days after the shooting in Paterson."

Richard has to be careful in his cross; he doesn't want to do anything that would give away the idea that Nick might have been kidnapped.

"Sergeant, how accurate are these GPS records?"

"In this case, I would say about thirty to forty yards in each direction."

"These were garden-apartment multiple units, correct?"

"Yes, sir."

"So how many homes would fit within that radius?"

"Impossible to say exactly, but most likely sixteen."

"Thank you. Do you know who murdered Russell Wheeler? Have the police arrested anyone?"

"I do not, and they have not."

"Do you know why he was murdered?"

"I do not, sir."

"Do you have any evidence it connects to this case?"

"I do not."

"Thank you."

Next up for me is George Truesdale, Nick's neighbor. I hesitated calling him because what he has to say isn't terribly compelling. But it could be relevant, and ultimately I decided it was better that the jury hear it than not.

Truesdale shows up in a suit and tie. The suit is a couple of sizes too small for him; he either hasn't worn it in years or he borrowed it from a person smaller than him.

I get him to tell the jury that he lives down the block from Nick, and that Nick would drive him to and from his job as a cashier not far from the Moore Law offices. On the day of the shooting, Nick did not pick him up, which was completely uncharacteristic.

"What did you do?" I asked.

"I called him, but got no answer, so I walked down to his house."

"Was he there?"

"No, but I saw a car coming out of the driveway next to his unit. It was a car I hadn't seen before."

"Who was driving?"

"Some guy who I didn't know; he looked really big, with a neck like a football player, you know? There was another guy in the car, but he was in the backseat, sitting on the left behind the driver. I remember I thought it was weird that he wasn't in the front."

I turn him over to Richard, who I actually think is salivating. But his face reflects annoyance that he has to deal with this nonsense.

"Mr. Truesdale, how many units use that driveway?"

"I don't know. Maybe eight? Ten?"

"Do you have the slightest idea that the car you saw had anything to do with Nick Williams?"

"Not really."

"Thank you, no further questions."

Truesdale leaves the stand probably thinking, *I got dressed up for this?*

It's rare for me at this late stage that I haven't fully decided on which witnesses I am going to call.

The potential witnesses that I am debating include Steven Loomis, Derek Shaffer, and Thomas Roden. All three are on my witness list and have received subpoenas.

The issue with Loomis is whether I want to share with the jury that Moore Law has been cheating certain clients by withholding part of their settlements. It would obviously show corruption, but doesn't directly tie into the shootings. Or if it does, I don't know how.

In the mind of the judge, it probably wouldn't even tie in indirectly, and he might rule it inadmissible. I think at this point that would be a correct ruling: if I don't know how the corruption relates to this trial, I don't see how the judge and the jury could.

But I do want Loomis to testify to his being attacked the other night. Any violence against employees of that firm, especially those from the Paterson office, works in Nick's favor since he was in jail at the time.

I'm annoyed at myself over a stupid mistake I made. I've learned that the two men who attacked Loomis have been released on bail. I should have had either Corey or Marcus there to follow them when they got out, but I didn't. It's the kind of unforced error that I can't afford to make.

The other two possible witnesses that I am debating with

myself over are ex-doctor Derek Shaffer and Chicago crime figure Thomas Roden. Shaffer is the more likely of the two, since
he has a direct tie to the law firm, while Roden does not. Where
they both connect to my case is that Wheeler called them the
night before he was killed.

It's a shaky connection, but it at least further muddies the
waters. Since we only have to show reasonable doubt, water
muddying is a positive.

In Shaffer's case, my instinct is that he is more likely to make
a mistake if I spring the Wheeler phone call on him. Just finding
out that he was on the witness list caused him to get Loomis to
call and berate me for doing it, after which he called me himself.

My hope would be that even though I'm not likely to get a
confession out of Shaffer, maybe he will look like a deer caught in
the headlights in front of the jury. Of course, I don't even know
what he would be confessing to.

I think my best move is to have Loomis and Shaffer testify,
but not Roden. When I get to court tomorrow morning, I will
ask Eddie to have the court send out notifications that they need
to be in court the next morning, first thing.

Now Eddie and I are meeting with Nick for an extended session of preparation for his testimony. I am still leery of him taking the stand, but that just reflects a defense attorney instinct.
I know of trials that were likely to go the defense's way but got
blown out of the water when the defendant testified.

Nick is nervous about it; if he wasn't, he would be a candidate
for an insanity defense. The rest of his life depends on his convincing the jury he is telling the truth. It's an incredible burden
for anyone, whether or not they are being honest.

By now I know, despite all my earlier doubts, that every word
of Nick's story is true.

I take Nick through what my questioning will be, and his

responses are fine. I caution him not to amplify or exaggerate; he should stick only to the facts. If not, Richard will have an opportunity to trip him up.

By the time he testifies, we will have more witnesses that will have provided additional corroboration, so the burden on Nick will not be quite so great. He won't realize that, though; he'll believe that everything is riding on what he says.

And he'll be right.

Eddie Dowd has been preparing Ben Lacey, the dog walker, for his testimony about the warehouse and believes that he will do well.

He'd better, because he is the key witness to link Nick to the warehouse in Newton where he was held prisoner.

Lacey and his wife have been staying in a hotel in East Rutherford and, according to Eddie, loving every minute of it. "He can't get over that there's a minibar," Eddie says, just before the session starts. "And that you can get room service until ten P.M. I don't want to see your bill."

"It will be worth it if he doesn't screw up." Then, "Did you serve the papers on Derek Shaffer?" They ordered Shaffer to appear at court tomorrow morning.

Eddie laughs. "I sure did. He went nuts; you'd think he was a linebacker I just did a crackback block on."

Judge Ramirez and the jury come in and I call Ben Lacey to the stand. He doesn't seem nervous; I think he's loving the attention.

I briefly take him through a mini-biography. He says that he was a custodian at Newton High School for thirty years, is now retired, and has been living with his wife in the same house for forty-one years.

I show him a photo of Russell Wheeler and ask him if he's ever seen him before.

"I sure have. He was standing outside a warehouse not too far from where I live. I walk my dog past there every day."

"When was this?"

"June twenty-ninth."

"How can you be sure of the date?"

"It was my birthday. I was going to meet my friend; we were having breakfast outside at the diner. He brought his dog also."

"Did you speak to the man in front of the warehouse?" I hold up the photo again. "This man?"

"Sure did. I was being friendly, but he told me to get lost. People don't talk that way where we live."

"He was just standing there?"

"Yeah, it was like he was guarding the place or something. But it's just this empty warehouse."

I show him a photo of the exterior of the warehouse, and he identifies it as the place where he saw and spoke to Wheeler. He also says that he saw Wheeler each of the next two days as well.

"Did you speak to him either time?"

"Nah, I stayed across the street. He was a scary guy."

I get Lacey to relate how I took him inside the warehouse and showed him one particular room. Then I show the photos he took of the room, making special mention of the hook in the wall and the darkened windows.

"Have you ever seen a hook like that, whether in your career as a building custodian, or at any other time or place?"

"No."

"Did I ask you to try and move this one, or pull it out of the wall?"

"Yeah. I couldn't budge it."

I turn him over to Richard, who asks if he ever saw Nick before today.

"Just on television. You know, they show his picture a lot."

"Was the man you saw carrying a weapon?"

"I didn't see one."

Richard introduces another photograph into evidence and shows it to Lacey. "So just to be sure, this is the man you saw?"

Lacey looks at it quickly and says, "That's him."

"Let the record show that this is a photograph of Frank Graziano, a lawyer in my office. No further questions."

It was an excellent move by Richard and was damaging to Lacey's credibility. But overall I think he did fairly well, and if he ate a hundred dollars' worth of macadamia nuts from the minibar, it was money well spent.

Next I call Steven Loomis. I'm sure he's worried that I am going to expose the fraud regarding settlement payments, but I'm not. At this point it's irrelevant and doesn't advance my position at all.

He identifies himself as the CEO of Moore Law, and I briefly have him describe the scope of the operation nationally, or at least in the eleven states they are in.

"Where is your personal office?"

"For now I'm working out of our Passaic office, but until the shootings I was based in Paterson."

"You haven't reopened that office?"

"We have not. We are still contemplating whether to move to a new Paterson office or just not have one at all. We will not be reopening that office. It doesn't feel right."

"You were not there the day of the shootings?"

He shakes his head. "I was not. I often take Fridays off in the summer."

"Did you know Nick Williams during his time in that office?"

"We certainly met a number of times; I wouldn't say I knew him well at all."

"Ever hear any complaints about him?"

"No."

"Did we have occasion to meet the other evening?"

"Yes."

"Please describe what led to that meeting."

"I was going to meet with a client in Montclair, at her house, to discuss a settlement issue. I arrived after dark, and on my way toward her front door, I was attacked by two men. One of them punched me in the side of the head, knocking me down.

"Then they grabbed me; I believe they were going to remove me from there. I don't know what their intention was, but I certainly believed my life was in danger."

"Yet you're here and apparently intact."

"Yes. One of your investigators, I later learned his name was Marcus Clark, showed up and rather forcefully disabled the two attackers, leaving them unconscious on the ground."

"Why was he there, if you know?"

"He was apparently following me, as part of your investigation."

"So just to recap, you were not at the office when a man came in and killed your employees. But subsequently, just recently, you were attacked by men who you believe may well have been out to kill you?"

"Yes."

"Did it enter your mind that perhaps you were meant to be a target when the others were killed, and that now they were finishing the job?"

"I don't know."

"But it's a reasonable possibility?"

Richard objects, saying that Loomis has already said he doesn't know. Ramirez sustains, and I end my questioning. I am sure Loomis must be relieved that the corruption did not come up.

I didn't avoid the topic because of any concern about him or his company. I think he's lying through his teeth when he denies that something bigger is going on.

The problem is that not only do I not know what that larger conspiracy is, but I can't even prove that there is one. The last thing I want to do is flounder around in front of the jury, ultimately getting nowhere.

In his cross-examination, Richard uses a similar approach to the one he's been going with, which is to appear dismissive of these irrelevancies. He asks Loomis if he knows why he was attacked.

"I do not."

"Could it have been a random mugging?"

"It's possible, but it did not feel like that."

"Were the men arrested?"

"Yes."

"Did you learn their names?"

"Yes."

"Had you ever heard of them?"

"No."

"Do you have any information that they were in any way attached to the shootings at your office, or to this case? I'm not asking for speculation, but actual information or evidence."

"I do not."

"Thank you."

Derek Shaffer's reaction was having the effect Andy Carpenter had hoped for.

He was extremely upset and worried; it was one thing to have been put on a witness list, but another to actually be called to the stand.

If Carpenter didn't know anything, why would he be calling him to testify? What did Shaffer have to do with the purpose of the trial, which was to determine who killed all those people? Shaffer was more than an arm's length from all of that; he had had nothing to do with giving the order.

The only person Shaffer could call about it was Thomas Roden. Shaffer didn't expect much comfort; Roden could do nothing about it.

"He can't know anything," Roden said when Shaffer told him the news.

"You can't possibly know that."

Roden knew that was true and was worried that Shaffer would say something stupid and revealing on the stand.

Secretly Roden was glad that he wasn't called to testify himself; it's possible that the session with Carpenter and his bodyguard, Marcus Clark, had had the desired effect. It hadn't gone well for Roden's people, but may still have convinced Carpenter to back off.

But that didn't mean Roden was confident in Shaffer. Shaffer was a genius at what he did, but in Roden's view was not nearly stable enough to be counted on.

Shaffer ended the call abruptly. He was angry and frustrated; Roden was going to stay above the fray and untouched, while he, Shaffer, was in serious danger.

Different people have different ways of finding time to think and clear their head. Shaffer's way was to go for a drive; he would spend the time anticipating what Carpenter might confront him with and come up with a counterstrategy.

He took comfort in that, at the end of the day, Carpenter could only have suspicions. If he had solid evidence of what had happened, Shaffer wouldn't be going to court tomorrow. He would be in jail.

He drove for almost four hours, including a stop for lunch. By the time he got home, he was feeling better about things. His initial panic was unwarranted; he could handle anything that Carpenter threw at him.

It turned out that Carpenter wasn't the person he had to worry about. When he got back, two men were waiting for him inside his home.

He had no idea how they got in, but that wasn't important.

He knew why they were there.

That Derek Shaffer is not here this morning shocks me.
He is not unsophisticated; he has to know that defying a subpoena will lead to significant consequences. That he has chosen to do that may well indicate that he's more afraid of being questioned under oath than he is of the justice system.

I ask for a session in the judge's chambers, out of earshot of both the jury and the people in the gallery. I want to talk about Shaffer's defiance of the subpoena, but I don't want to do so publicly because I don't want to alert him about our next steps.

Once Richard and I are alone with Judge Ramirez, I tell him what has happened. He promises to alert the police immediately, so that they can find Shaffer. The judge will issue a contempt citation and take action against Shaffer once he determines that Shaffer is not ill or does not have another valid reason for not showing up.

Because it will be a while before that determination can be made, I ask Judge Ramirez to grant a continuance until tomorrow. At that point, either Shaffer will be here, or I will wrap up the case with my final witness.

Richard does a half double take at my last comment. He's been wondering whether Nick will take the stand, and he would obviously love to know if what I said means that last witness will be Nick.

As a good attorney, he will prepare for Nick regardless; the last thing he would want is for Nick to testify with Richard unprepared to cross-examine.

Nick is taken back to the jail, but Eddie and I wait in an anteroom for word on Shaffer. After about an hour, we head down to the cafeteria for coffee. They have only packaged muffins; I would give anything for a piece of Hilda's babka.

The muffins taste like soft cardboard, but I'm hungry and bored so I have two of them. Eddie, who is one of those annoying people who are opposed to putting garbage in their body, has only coffee.

We're about ready to go back when one of the bailiffs comes to get us. He says that Judge Ramirez wants us in his chambers right away.

This time I bring Eddie with me, and when we arrive, the judge and Richard are both waiting. Also there is Lieutenant Angela Courtney of the Paterson PD. Judge Ramirez introduces us to Lieutenant Courtney, who I assume is here to update us on the Shaffer situation. I doubt very much that Richard has heard anything yet; it would be bad form to have discussed this with one side and not the other.

"Myself and two other officers went to Mr. Shaffer's house. He did not answer the doorbell, so having probable cause of a crime . . . that being the defiance of a lawful subpoena . . . we entered the premises.

"Mr. Shaffer was not at home, nor was anyone else there. We executed a quick search. It was difficult to tell if Mr. Shaffer had become a fugitive; certainly there was no evidence that he took a significant amount of clothing with him."

This is stunning news, and potentially very damaging to our case. Yet I can't say it is surprising; Roden has shown a total willingness to eliminate whoever might be a threat to him. He obviously saw Shaffer and his testimony as dangerous.

"Toiletries were still in the bathroom, though of course he could have had a separate set to travel. The bed was not slept in. There was a full pot of cold coffee; we determined that the coffee maker was automatic and went off at seven A.M.

"One thing clearly unusual was in what appeared to be his office. I would say that he had an elaborate computer setup, based on the wiring, laser printer, and other devices that would complement such a setup.

"However, the computer itself was gone. Once again there are limited conclusions to be reached, based on current knowledge of Mr. Shaffer's situation, but my best guess is that he left and took the computer with him.

"That's all I can tell you at this time."

"So what is your assessment of the situation?" Judge Ramirez asks.

"That he left last night, but voluntarily or not, it's hard to say. The missing computer would indicate to me that he is not planning to return anytime soon, though once again our knowledge is limited. It's possible that the computer could be in for repair."

Judge Ramirez says, "Thank you. I am issuing a bench warrant for his arrest." He turns to Richard and me. "I won't be extending the continuance beyond today." That is no surprise to me. "Be prepared to resume the defense case tomorrow, whether or not Mr. Shaffer shows up."

"He won't show up," I say. "He's dead."

Richard does a double take, and Judge Ramirez asks, "Do you have any information or knowledge to support that opinion?"

I smile. "Nothing that would be admissible in court, Your Honor."

Thomas Roden is clearly calling all the shots, literally and figuratively.

Starting with Charles Brisker and moving on to Russell Wheeler and Derek Shaffer, he seems to be removing any possible links between himself and the conspiracy. He attempted to include Steven Loomis on the elimination list, but Marcus thwarted that.

Roden has obviously concluded that whatever the conspiracy is, it is effectively over. Roden provided the muscle and the ruthlessness necessary to keep it going, but the nuts and bolts of it had to be in the hands of Loomis, Brisker, and Shaffer.

If all three of them have been removed, it's done.

These are just my best guesses; since I don't know what's going on, I can't accurately assess its status.

It's extremely frustrating to me that Loomis will not come clean. His likely two main coconspirators, Brisker and Shaffer, are dead. The third one, Roden, tried to have Loomis killed. Yet he won't talk.

I'm sure the reason for his silence is that to reveal the conspiracy is to incriminate himself in something so terrible that he would go to prison, probably for a long time. His best chance, he probably figures, is to remain silent and come up with some truce with Roden.

Good luck with that.

Another thing I don't know is why the conspiracy unraveled. Obviously the shooting at the law firm was the beginning of the end for whatever was going on, but what prompted Roden to take such a drastic step?

My best guess is that Brisker was posing some kind of a danger. Maybe he was conscience-stricken and was threatening to reveal all. His daughter, Karen, said that he was terribly worried about something in the days before he died. Maybe he knew that when he went to law enforcement, he would be in danger legally, and physically from Roden's people.

The most frustrating part of this, besides my inability to use any of this to help in Nick's defense, is that what Roden has done has worked. He is essentially untouchable; absent Loomis's testimony, he has succeeded in insulating himself from law enforcement.

Shaffer is particularly puzzling to me. I just do not know where he could have fit in to all this. Loomis described him as a medical consultant to the firm, which may or may not have been true. But it's hard to imagine that just one person was the contact with hospitals and insurance companies throughout the eleven states that the law firm operated in.

I'm assuming Shaffer has been killed, though I don't know for sure. The apparent hastiness of his departure could have just reflected a reluctance to testify, but I doubt it. This has the feel of Roden's handiwork.

If Shaffer did not leave voluntarily, as I suspect, then his killers taking his computer is an interesting development. Something incriminating must have been on there, something that could have led back to Roden. Or at least the bad guys recognized that danger and took the computer to make sure.

But maybe there's a way around that.

When I get to court, I ask Eddie to arrange for us to have access to Shaffer's apartment. I also ask him to tell Sam to stand by, that I will call him during the lunch break, after Nick's direct-examination testimony.

I'll either be in a good mood or very bad mood by then.

I can tell that Nick is nervous as he's brought into court.

By this point I can read his moods pretty well; I just hope the jury hasn't learned to do it. Any fair-minded and intelligent person would understand his anxiety as normal, and not as an indication of guilt. It remains to be seen how fair-minded and intelligent this jury is.

"You okay?" I ask.

He nods. "I think so."

"You've got a big advantage. You're telling the truth; that makes it much easier. Just stick to the absolute truth; don't worry how you think it's playing for the jury. You'll be fine."

He nods, but it's not a nod that says, *Dammit, Andy, you're right. I'm going to slam-dunk this thing!*

Richard is walking toward me, so I get up to meet him halfway. "You going to put your boy on the stand?"

"Coming right up."

"Damn, I should have prepared for it." He smiles.

I don't get a chance to respond because Judge Ramirez comes in. We take our seats, he calls in the jury, and I call Nick Williams to the stand.

"How long did you work at Moore Law?" is my first question.

"About seven months."

I get him to list his responsibilities and say that he liked his coworkers a great deal; he considered them friends.

"Did you make as much money as you wanted to?"

He smiles. "No, I wanted to make more. But Mr. Brisker explained to me that company policy was that I had to wait a year. He said he was sorry, but that there was nothing he could do."

"Please describe what you did on the day that the shootings took place."

Nick nods. "I got up and prepared to go to work, like I did every day. I went out the back door, because that's where my garage is. I think I remember being grabbed from behind, but that's all, and I'm not even positive about that."

"What is the next thing you remember?"

"Waking up in a room, an empty room with no furniture. There was one window, but it was black; it looked like it was covered up from the outside. It was all the way on the other side of the room.

"There was a large, closed hook embedded into a wall, it was about five feet high. My left leg was shackled . . . there was a chain . . . and it connected to that hook. There was also a bathroom about five feet from where the hook was."

"Did you try and pull the hook out of the wall, or somehow disconnect the chain from either the wall or your leg?"

"Boy, did I ever. But I couldn't do either; not even close."

"Did you try to break the window?"

He shakes his head. "The chain wasn't long enough for me to get over there."

I once again show the photos of the room to Nick and the jury, and he says that it looks exactly like where he was held.

"What happened next?"

"After I tried everything I could think of, I just sat there. I was really scared; I didn't know if anyone was going to show up. I was afraid they would and I was probably more afraid they wouldn't."

"Did anyone show up?"

He nods. "Yes. Two men, one really big and one about my size. They had ski masks over their faces."

"What did they do?"

"They brought me food and told me if I behaved myself, I wouldn't get hurt. The big guy called me 'friend.'"

"Do you think you knew them?"

Nick shakes his head. "No, but I can't be sure. I didn't recognize their voices."

"How long were you there?"

"Hard to know, but I would guess three or four days. After I woke up, they came twice a day and brought me food. Then, the last day, they put a hood over my head, unchained me, and took me out of there. I was afraid they were going to kill me."

I'm pleased with Nick's testimony so far. He comes off as appropriately nervous, but sincere. Of course, the jury might have a completely different opinion.

"What did they do?"

"They put me on the floor of a car in the back and drove me to a rest stop on the Garden State Parkway. They gave me a cell phone and told me to call the police and turn myself in."

"Did they say why you should turn yourself in?"

"No, I had no idea what they were talking about."

"So what did you do?"

"I called my friend Marcus Clark. He came and picked me up and brought me to you. He also told me the horrible news about the office. You told me to turn myself in, so I did."

Nick has done an outstanding job; he's told the story truthfully with no embellishment, leaving Richard little to attack. The jury will either believe him, or they won't.

"So you don't know who took you?" Richard asks.

"No."

"You don't know what they did to knock you out?"

"No."

"You don't know where they took you, in terms of location?"

"I do now, but I didn't then."

"You don't know how long you were held?"

"Not really."

"You don't know why you were held?"

"I can't be sure. Now it seems like it must have been so that I would be blamed for the deaths."

"You don't know how the murder weapon was found near your house with your fingerprints on it?"

"No."

"Do you know how the killer knew his way around the office and knew Sally Montrose's nickname?"

"No."

"So your alibi is that you have no idea about anything?"

"I've told the truth."

"Do you know your way around that office?"

"Yes."

"Finally an answer other than no."

I object and Judge Ramirez strikes the comment.

Then, "Let's try for some more yeses. Do you know Sally Montrose's nickname to be Monty?"

"Yes."

"Do you have a tattoo of a hook on your arm?"

"Yes."

"Do you have sneakers with red and yellow stripes on them?"

"Yes."

"Did you get turned down when you applied for a raise?"

"Yes."

Richard shakes his head as if disdainful of what he has heard. "No further questions."

I think Richard did not do much damage, though he covered all the ground available to him. It's up to the jury to decide whether Nick is telling the truth.

"Your Honor, the defense rests."

Sam, Derek Shaffer has disappeared with his computer. Eddie has just arranged for us to get access."

"Disappeared voluntarily?" Sam asks.

"Not sure, but I don't think he'll ever get a taste of Hilda's babka."

"So bad guys took his computer?"

"Apparently. Let me ask you a question; you said he had excellent protections on his consultant-company data. You couldn't break into it."

"Right."

"So he must be computer savvy?"

"Either he or someone who works for him. Maybe he has a great IT guy."

"Either way, he would back everything up, right? Whatever was on his computer would be backed up somewhere?"

"Of course."

"Where?"

"Are we talking about data that could show criminality?"

"We are."

"Then I doubt it would be in the cloud. Law enforcement could get the provider to give it to them with a warrant. So I would say a separate hard drive; possibly more than one."

"Where would he keep them? In his house?"

"I would think at least one would be there. He might keep

another one off premises, maybe in a safe-deposit box, in case there was a fire in his house."

"Eddie has arranged for us to get access. I want you to go there and see if you can find it. You can bring the Brigade with you if you want them to help you look. You have his address?"

"Of course."

"Will it be password protected?"

"Definitely. Depending on the password, I might be able to break it. I have a program that tests thousands of passwords a minute."

"So you mean whether you can break it depends on the number of characters, that kind of thing?"

"I'll give you an example. If it's seven characters and includes numbers, upper- and lowercase letters and symbols, my program can crack it in six minutes. If it's fourteen characters of just upper- and lowercase letters, it would take eight hundred and sixty-seven thousand years."

"Then let's hope it's not the latter; the jury won't be out that long."

"First we have to find it."

"Also, call Marcus and ask him to go with you, just in case you're not the only people interested in searching that house."

"I can handle myself."

"I know, but I suspect it's been a while since Hilda and Eli have been in a gunfight."

"Okay, I'll call Marcus."

First of all, I want to thank you for what you have already done," Richard says as he begins his closing argument.

The courtroom has an electric feeling today; this is the culmination. Laurie is here in the front row, as is Nick's friend Rafe. He's been here a few times during the trial, whenever work permitted.

Richard continues, "You've had to hear disturbing testimony and see very unpleasant images, and you've had to listen patiently as we lawyers drone on. I know how dull I can be; my wife frequently reminds me.

"But what you have done so far, and especially what you are about to do, is crucially important. It is the bedrock of our entire justice system: the accused are judged by his or her peers. And that is what you are about to do; you will make a judgment, a decision, about the guilt or innocence of Nicholas Williams.

"So what Mr. Carpenter and I have been doing all these days is preparing you to make that decision. In this case, I would submit that it is all about knowledge, about what we know and can prove, and about what Mr. Williams does not know.

"We know that a man came into the Moore Law office, with a loaded gun, and killed six people. He was disguised, but Sally Montrose knew who he was.

"We know that he knew her nickname, we know that he wore

identical sneakers to the ones Mr. Williams always wore, and we know he had an identical tattoo in the same place on his body as Mr. Williams.

"We know that Laura Schauble also saw the tattoo and the sneakers, and that they both believed the voice belonged to Mr. Williams. We know that Ms. Montrose said that the gunman walked upright in a rather unique manner, the same as Mr. Williams.

"We further know that the killer knew his way around the office as he calmly and methodically located each person to gun down.

"We know that none of this could be a coincidence.

"We also know that the murder weapon, with Mr. Williams's fingerprints on it, was found discarded not far from his house. Not in his own dumpster, or in his house, where someone who was planting it might have left it. No, six houses away, where it might have gone undetected.

"Now, let's talk about what Mr. Williams does not know. He claims to have been kidnapped, but he doesn't know who did it. He doesn't know why they did it. He didn't know where they took him. He doesn't know how long they held him. And he doesn't know how the murder weapon ended up near his house.

"So you are left with the choice of believing what we know, what you know from the evidence, or what Mr. Williams does not know. I would submit that decision is easier than most of the ones I run into in my profession.

"This was a horrible crime, maybe the worst I've seen in my career. Nothing you can do can bring back those six souls, but you can give them some semblance of justice. And you can prevent Nick Williams from ever hurting another person again.

"I hope and trust you will do that."

I think Richard has done a good job, particularly at the end.

Jurors do not want to think that they could be letting someone go, only to have them kill again. They do not want that blood on their hands.

"Like Mr. Wallace, I would like to thank you for performing a very difficult service," I say, matching Richard pander for pander. "You have been attentive and serious and respectful and dedicated, and we could not ask for anything more.

"And that, ladies and gentlemen, is the only thing that Mr. Wallace and I agree on.

"There are definitely things that Mr. Williams does not know; he was quite open about that. But when you are knocked out and locked in a room for three days without contact with the outside world, that becomes more understandable.

"Fortunately, we don't have to rely solely on Mr. Williams's recollections. We have independent confirmation of so many of them. For instance, we have phone records which show someone present at his house at the time he was leaving for work. And that was not just anyone, and certainly not a benign presence.

"It was a murderer, Russell Wheeler, who was then placed by an eyewitness at the location where Mr. Williams was held. What was he doing there? Was he just hanging out in Newton, New Jersey? Does that make sense?

"And then we have a neighbor of Mr. Williams, who saw a strange car with people he did not recognize, leaving Mr. Williams's driveway that morning. One of them drove and the other sat in the back. Could the man in the back have been watching their prisoner? Is that a reasonable possibility?

"And how did Mr. Williams get around all this time if his car was in the garage with an odometer that showed it had not been driven? And how did he get to the rest stop? If he drove, where was the car? Did Mr. Wallace present any evidence to show that a cab or Uber dropped him off? No, and you can bet he searched for it.

"And why did the killer deliberately show his tattoo, or wear distinctive sneakers that could be recognized, yet he wore a mask covering his face? And why and how did he go back to his house to leave the murder weapon in an incriminating place?

"And while we're asking why, why did the killer not shoot Ms. Montrose? Was he really distracted, or did he want a witness that would identify the killer as Mr. Williams, based on the tattoo and sneakers and use of her nickname?

"And did you hear from Mr. Wallace any reason for Mr. Williams to have killed five of his friends and a stranger? Because he was going to have to wait five more months for a raise, as was company policy? Does that seem logical to you?

"I am here to tell you that Nick Williams was set up for this crime, and every single word you heard during this trial is consistent with that. Let me repeat that . . . *Every. Single. Word.*

"You may think I am wrong when I say that, but there is no way on earth that you could know that I am wrong. This courtroom is knee-deep in reasonable doubt.

"What happened in that office that day was a nightmare. What Mr. Williams has gone through since that day is another nightmare, a living one. I would not wish it on anyone.

"But you can end it. You can give Nick Williams his life back. I hope and believe that you will."

I walk back to the defense table with that sick feeling I always get after my closing argument. It's now out of my control, and we have to depend on twelve strangers to do the right thing. I'm not sure I've met twelve strangers in my entire life that I can count on to do the right thing.

But it is what it is.

I shake Nick's hand and he thanks me. Judge Ramirez gives his instructions to the jury and then adjourns court for the day.

I'm walking to my car when my cell rings. It's Sam, and his first words are "Hilda found the hard drive. It was in his night-table drawer; it wasn't even locked."

"Can you break the password?"

"Haven't tried yet. Is it okay if we take it back to the office?"

"Not yet. Get a subpoena for it, and then have Eddie contact Tina Winston." Sam knows her; she's the state police cop in the cybercrime division who has already testified in the trial.

I continue, "I want her involved; maybe she can make a copy of the hard drive and you can work off of that. I leave that to you computer geeks. But I want to preserve the chain of custody."

"Geeks?"

"Sorry. Experts. Just let me know when you get the password."

"If we get the password."

've been wrong all along in my approach to taking on clients.

Because I'm wealthy and lazy and want to work as little as possible, for years I have taken the position that I would only represent people that I believed to be innocent. For a while I thought I violated that in this case, but because of Marcus I made an exception. Then it turned out that Nick was innocent after all.

But the truth is that I should not be representing innocent clients in the first place.

When you have an innocent client, you dread the possibility that he or she might be convicted. Speaking for myself, I am filled with panic that I could not get a jury to see the truth, and that an innocent person might go to prison because of my failings.

But with a guilty client, if I lose, I lose. The creep got what he deserved; he committed the crime so he'll do the time.

Bottom line . . . innocent clients are the worst . . . guilty clients are the way to go. And the guiltier the better.

It's been three days since the jury started deliberating and one day since they called us all to the courtroom to say they were deadlocked on all counts. Judge Ramirez did what judges always do in these situations: he told them to go back and keep working toward a verdict.

I have no idea what the vote has been like, but I'm not surprised that they're having trouble deciding. I think we've made a good reasonable-doubt case, but I can see where some of them might take the government's evidence as gospel.

We are asking them to believe a complicated scenario; the prosecution is asking them to take eyewitness testimony at face value.

I'm in my typical high-anxiety verdict-waiting mode. I don't hang around with other people during this time, except for Laurie and Ricky. It's easy for me to stay apart from friends; they know what I'm like at this time and have no interest in being near me.

Adding to my frustration is that Sam has not yet been able to break the password and get into Shaffer's hard drive. Sam keeps telling me that it could come at any time, or it could be never. We won't know until we know.

Thanks, Sam.

Of course, for all I know the computer could be filled with photos of Shaffer's last vacation. All that is certain is that whoever did him in was concerned that the computer contained incriminating evidence, or they wouldn't have taken it.

Even if Sam gets into it, the timing is not going to work for the trial. The jury is going to come to a decision soon, even if the result is that they can't come to a decision.

Most defense attorneys usually hope for a hung jury. It's better than a conviction, and the government might choose not to retry the case. It often depends on the vote count; if conviction was close, they go forward again.

But in this case, with a crime of this magnitude and media attention, it is hard to see the case not retried. That means Nick will be in jail for a long time, regardless of the ultimate outcome, which horrifies me.

Did I mention that guilty clients are the way to go?

My knowledge of whatever was going on at Moore Law has not increased over time. I know that they were cheating their clients, and I'm quite sure that Charles Brisker and Steven Loomis were behind it, but that's the extent of it. I still cannot picture that being a reason for mass murder.

Laurie makes hamburgers and french fries for dinner. She makes the fries in an air fryer, but they are surprisingly good. The best part is that I can make mine as burnt as I want.

In the last couple of days I've played Ricky two games of video-game college football to get my mind off things, and he's beaten me by a combined score of 63–14. He apparently has no interest in making me feel better.

After dinner Ricky challenges me to another game, and I accept. I'm going to try a new strategy this time; I'm going to beg him for mercy.

The new strategy doesn't work; he's up 27–0 at the half. But I have found a flaw in the game and I raise it with him, hoping that it will give me a loophole to take away his lead so we can start over.

"The clock is stopping after a first down. That rule has been changed; it only stops in the last two minutes of the half and game."

"I think you're wrong."

"About college football? Never."

"The computer wouldn't show the rule if it wasn't right."

"So you believe the computer over your own father?"

"Sorry, Dad. No offense, but I always go by the computer."

Something about the way he says this hits me, and suddenly I'm not thinking about college football or video games or even the verdict wait. Suddenly I think I might know what the hell is going on.

Ricky must see a weird look on my face because he says, "You okay, Dad? Maybe you're right about the rule."

"Doesn't matter, Rick . . . doesn't matter at all, as long as I'm right about something else."

place a call to Sally Montrose, and once again she takes the call.

"You are nothing if not persistent."

"People have said worse things about me. Can we meet? I need to talk to you."

"What about?"

"I think I may have stumbled upon something, and knowing what you do about how your company operates, you could either confirm it or steer me in the right direction."

"I don't know . . ." She's obviously reluctant.

"I promise it's the last time I bother you. I have to be near court today; can we meet near there? Maybe this afternoon?"

"I can't. I'm going back into work today."

"You decided to go back?"

"Not officially. I'm going in to see how it feels. I'm gearing myself up for not seeing my friends."

"'Empty Chairs at Empty Tables,'" I say, referencing a song from *Les Misérables* that is about losing all your friends and the guilt of survival.

I doubt she's familiar with it, or maybe she doesn't think it worth responding to, because she says, "What about tonight?"

"Tonight works."

"Can we do the parking-lot thing again? I doubt Steven Loomis would react well to my talking to you."

"Sure."

We make arrangements to meet in the parking lot of the Bergen Town Center tonight at 8:00 P.M. I take the dogs on a long walk through Eastside Park. My cell phone is in my pocket and I know it can ring at any time, telling me the jury is back.

I hope it rings, and I hope it doesn't ring.

I call Sam and ask the key question: "Sam, if I send you an email from my phone and another from my computer, can you tell which is which?"

"You mean can I tell what type of device an email comes from?"

"Yes."

"Of course."

"By looking at it?" I ask.

"No, by researching the header. There are sites that let you . . . you sure you want all these details?"

"Actually I don't. I just want to make sure you can do it."

"I can do it."

"Excellent." I tell Sam what I want him to do, and that I need it as soon as possible, meaning within a few hours. He promises to get it done, so I end the call so he can go to work on it.

Next I go to the discovery documents and retrieve the file of Brisker's emails. It confirms what I expected, but I'm going to need Sam to seal the deal.

My final move is to call Karen Brisker, Charles's daughter. "You said you had lunch with your father on the day he died."

"Yes."

"What time was that?"

"I'm not sure. Probably at twelve thirty, maybe one o'clock."

"How long would lunch have lasted?"

"At least an hour; more likely an hour and a half. Why?"

"I can't say now, but I will very soon."

She lets me off the phone without pressing me further.

When I get off the call, I take Tara and Hunter for another walk, mostly so I can figure out what to do next.

I've asked Tara repeatedly how she thinks the verdict will go, and she gives me absolutely nothing. I understand she doesn't want to build my hopes up or depress me. But I would at least like some response, and just sniffing shrubbery or pissing on the grass does not cut it. When this is over, she and I are going to have a talk about what I expect of her.

"Tara, I don't think—"

The sentence is interrupted by the dreaded ringing of the cell phone, and caller ID drives it home; the call is coming from the courthouse.

"Andy?" It's Rita Gordon, the court clerk.

"The jury is back?"

"Yes, they want you down here at eleven A.M."

"Is there a verdict?"

"I don't know."

I turn around and take Tara and Hunter home. Laurie is waiting for me, and after I get dressed, we go down to the courthouse together. I don't say a word the entire way, except for "You've got a stop sign." Laurie isn't great at noticing stop signs.

We arrive and I take my seat at the defense table. Eddie is already here, and Nick is brought in a few minutes later.

Richard starts walking over and I meet him halfway. "I think they're hung," he says. I don't think he would say that without good reason, but there's always a chance that he's wrong.

Judge Ramirez calls the jury in, and the foreman immediately confirms that they are hung. The judge thanks the jury for their efforts and then says that he has no option but to declare a mistrial.

I know I should be relatively pleased with this outcome, but I am not. It likely means that Nick is going to spend a significant time in jail, no matter how this plays out.

I meet Richard halfway again and he says, "We fought the good fight."

"Don't retry it, Richard. The guy is innocent."

"Let's see what the vote was. But in a case like this, you know it won't be my decision, and the pressure to go through it again is going to be great. They won't just throw up their hands and say six people are dead but we can't nail someone for it."

They let Eddie and me talk to Nick for a few minutes after the adjournment. He has a lot of questions, none of which I can adequately answer. Finally he smiles and says, "Could have been worse."

"That's for sure," I say, and the bailiff comes to lead him away.

In the back of the courtroom the foreman and two other jurors are conducting a press conference of sorts. I walk over and ask one of the media members in the back if they said how they voted.

He nods. "Seven to five for conviction."

I walk away; I don't need to hear any more. It looks like we're going to have to go through this again.

'm sitting in my car at the back of the Bergen Town Center parking lot when Sally Montrose's car pulls up.

We didn't actually have to do it all the way back here because at this hour the mall is closed, so only three or four other cars are in the entire lot.

Sally parks next to me, gets out, and opens my door, sliding into the passenger seat. After we exchange hellos, she asks, "Can we do this quickly? I've had an exhausting day."

"How was getting back to work?"

"Difficult, but I think necessary. I'm glad I did it. What did you want to ask me about?"

"Filing cabinets and emails."

"What does that mean?"

"You had large filing cabinets moved into the office next to you, even though a new lawyer was starting and moving into that office a few days later."

"So? I told you, Laura and I were working together; this made it easier."

"Your offices were not that big; we're not talking about Madison Square Garden. She could have walked a few feet, but you wanted her there because you needed her as a witness."

"You're accusing me of something? Of being involved in what happened?"

I ignore the question. "Moving right along, the email that

Charles Brisker supposedly sent, asking people to stay late that day . . . he didn't send it. You did."

"I think I've heard enough of this garbage."

"It was sent at one ten in the afternoon. He was at lunch."

"So? He must have sent it from there on his phone."

"No, he didn't. It came from a computer, not a phone. You sent it from his account."

"You have no evidence for any of this."

"Whenever Brisker sent an email, he copied himself. I've checked out dozens of them. But on that particular email, he didn't. That's because you didn't want him to see it."

"Ridiculous," she says, but I can see the worry on her face.

I smile. "Which brings me to Derek Shaffer."

"What about him?"

"We found his backup hard drive."

"What does that have to do with me?"

"Turns out you're all over it. He typed your name so many times your ears must have been burning," I say, lying through my teeth.

"What are you trying to say?"

"That not only are you responsible for the financial fraud, but a hell of a lot of murders as well. And as you know, I'm not just talking about the mass shooting."

"You're out of your mind."

"Very possibly true, but I'm right about this. You sent the instructions to the banks in Charles Brisker's name. You shared everything; you had access to his emails. When you sent the email from Charles telling the people in the office to stay late that day, you killed people who were supposed to be your friends."

"None of this is true. I don't care what is on that hard drive, or what stupid theories you have."

"So here's where we are. You have until noon tomorrow afternoon to turn yourself in and tell what you know."

"Why would I possibly do that? You're just grasping at straws here."

"You didn't let me finish my thought. If you don't turn yourself in, I am going to make sure that Thomas Roden finds out that you ratted him out. And I'll put in enough details for him to be positive it's true. In that case, I've checked the actuarial tables at some of the insurance companies you ripped off, and your life expectancy would be about an hour and a half."

"You're serious about this."

"What tipped you off?"

She frowns. "I'm sorry about this, but I needed to take precautions just in case something like this happened." She opens the window about six inches and yells out, "Darrell!"

What happens next is beyond shocking, even though I expected something like it to happen. The Darrell she is talking about appears; he literally comes flying, landing on the front window and hood of the car.

His face crashes onto the window with a splat, and blood spurts from his nose. I don't think he's upset about his nose in the moment because he is clearly unconscious.

Montrose screams, which does not improve her position at all. Then she screams again, albeit less loudly, when Marcus appears at the passenger window.

"I assume that is Darrell on the hood? The guy with the smashed face?" I ask.

She doesn't answer, so I say, "I thought precautions were a good idea also. So we're back where we were. You've got until noon tomorrow to turn yourself in, and if you don't do it, Thomas Roden will deal with you. And I suspect he'll be sending someone better than Darrell.

"Oh, and just to make your decision easier, I taped this conversation on my phone."

"Andy, I—"

I interrupt, "Get out of my car, you piece of shit. Leave Darrell here; we'll deal with him."

So she does just that, leaving my car and walking to hers. Marcus watches her the entire time; it's always possible she has a handgun in the glove compartment. But all she does is start the car and drive away; this meeting didn't quite go the way she wanted it to.

Marcus takes Darrell off the front hood; he's slowly coming to, so Marcus puts him in handcuffs. Marcus throws him in the backseat of his car, and I tell him that I'll follow him to the police station.

I use the windshield-wiper fluid to try to clean the blood off the window, but it still leaves a few disgusting red smears. It's not the kind of things lawyers generally have to deal with.

We drive down to the police station. I've asked Laurie and Corey to meet us there; between them they are likely to know whatever detectives are on duty.

Sure enough, when we arrive, Corey is chatting away with one of them; they are apparently basketball-playing buddies. Darrell gets arrested; he was armed and getting ready to attack me when Marcus intervened. That charge might not stick, but there will be others, and after getting medical treatment on his face, he will wind up in a cell.

Marcus answers a few questions and then disappears; I don't even get a chance to thank him. I'm just glad I asked him to be at the parking lot, just in case. Left to deal with Darrell on my own, I suspect the result would have been somewhat different.

Darrell was out on bail for the kidnapping or mugging attempt on Steven Loomis at Cynthia Bullock's house; and this time he'll stay locked up.

I head home with Laurie; she had come to the station with Corey in his car. She drives while I call Richard Wallace and Pete Stanton at their respective homes.

I ask them both to meet me in Pete's office tomorrow morning. Richard agrees and doesn't question me on the subject of the meeting. He knows I wouldn't be making the request if it wasn't something important.

Pete is somewhat less respectful. He mentions something about me being an asshole. He ultimately goes along with the request, but threatens to strangle me if it turns out I'm wasting his time.

He's a heck of a guy.

start the meeting off by playing the tape of my conversation in the car with Sally Montrose.

Pete and Richard both listen intently; Pete hasn't even insulted me since I arrived, probably because Richard is here. Pete is trying to act like an adult, though it's a stretch for him.

When the tape is finished, Richard asks me to play it again, and I do. Once again they listen carefully, and this time Richard even takes a few notes, even though he obviously knows I'll be happy to let him copy it.

"What was that crashing noise?" Pete asks.

"It was Marcus shot-putting Darrell onto the front of the car."

Pete just nods in response. He's not surprised; he's familiar with Marcus's human-shot-putting prowess.

"You want to fill in the gaps?" Richard asks.

"Yes. To start off, most importantly, Nick Williams did not commit those murders. Every word that he said on the stand was true. I believe our friend Darrell, who Marcus tossed onto the windshield of my car, was the shooter.

"There were a number of very large malpractice settlements that Moore Law won, not just in New Jersey but probably in all eleven states that they practice in. In most of the cases their client did not receive all the money they were due, sometimes three or four hundred thousand dollars less.

"We notified a few of them about this discrepancy, and they

did not seem particularly surprised or upset. Cynthia Bullock is included in this group."

"She got less than she was supposed to?" Richard asks.

I nod. "Three hundred grand."

"Why was she okay with that?"

"Because she was paying to have her husband murdered. That was the going rate for buying hits in this operation."

"You're going to need to explain that further," Richard says.

"Happy to. Let's stick with Cynthia Bullock. She got to Thomas Roden . . . I'm not sure how . . . and she hired him to kill her husband, Gerald. By the way, they had already filed for divorce.

"But this was no ordinary hit. They made sure he got sick; it was easy to do. They slipped *E. coli* bacteria into his food, either in a restaurant or more likely at home. That sent him to the hospital.

"Derek Shaffer, may he rest in something other than peace, was the key player. Not only was he a doctor, but he was a computer whiz. He had lost his license by breaking into computers and placing digital opioid prescriptions years ago. This time he was upping his game.

"He broke into hospital systems, the hospitals where the targets had been taken. In Gerald Bullock's case, it was Montclair General. He caused mistakes, which in turn caused people to die. Bullock was deathly allergic to all antibiotics in the penicillin family, and he removed that information from his computer chart, so he was treated with it.

"The hospital administrator told me that it must have been inputted wrong, and that people just naturally follow what the computer tells them. But it wasn't inputted wrong; Shaffer sabotaged it.

"The hits weren't done to collect life insurance; they were

done to collect malpractice settlements. So since none of them looked like murder, there was no one to suspect. Part of the deal was that the plaintiffs hire Moore Law, so that they could manipulate the money.

"Cops are smart; not all of them are like Pete here. But there was no police involvement in these cases because no one thought it was murder. The hospitals and doctors were even admitting fault, they were in effect paying for these hits. It was brilliant."

"What tipped you off to this?"

"Ricky told me to trust the computer, which is what the people working in the hospitals did. And the victims that day trusted that the email came from Charles Brisker, because that's what the computer said."

"But you can't prove all this?" Richard asks. "Because the tape of your conversation doesn't get it done. Montrose really didn't admit anything."

"I know. Right now I can only prove the financial-fraud piece, not the murders. I'm betting that Montrose turns herself in and fills in the blanks, hoping to make a deal."

"And if she doesn't?" Pete asks.

"Then it will all come crashing down on them when Sam breaks the password."

"How long will that take?" Richard asks.

"It could take eight hundred and sixty-seven thousand years."

You want the good news or the bad news?" Richard asks when he calls me.

It's a question I hate because the bad always seems to outweigh the good. "Start with the good."

"Sally Montrose turned herself in; she's in custody and is being arraigned on Thursday."

"And the bad?"

"She didn't go anywhere near describing the conspiracy you laid out. She admitted being aware of the financial fraud, and being complicit in it. But she claimed it was orchestrated by Steven Loomis and Charles Brisker."

"Loomis and Brisker had nothing to do with it. When Brisker suspected it, he was killed. Then as Loomis got close, they went after him also."

"That's not how Montrose describes it," Richard says. "She half threw Derek Shaffer under the bus by saying that he was involved in manipulating the medical malpractice cases with Loomis and Brisker, but she wasn't really sure how, and she says she certainly knew nothing about any murders."

"So how do you read this?"

"Well, if we assume you're right about all this, and that's a pretty big if, then I think she wants to remain in custody for a while. At least until it blows over and Thomas Roden will move on. On the fraud charges she is not going to get a lot of jail time, if any."

"She played it smart. I should have anticipated it."

"Andy, based on what we have, I'm going to have no choice but to retry our case."

"I understand. When are we looking at?"

"I'll try to make it as soon as possible, but it will be up to the judge. I don't see it happening fast, but it will be less than eight hundred and sixty-seven thousand years."

"That's comforting."

"One other thing. Derek Shaffer's body was found last night, floating in the Passaic River."

"I'm going to miss his wit."

ndy, it's Hilda. Sam's not in yet, but there's something I thought you would want to know."

I clear the fog from my eyes and look at the clock; it's five thirty in the morning. "Hilda, is everything all right? Are you and Eli okay?"

"Fine. We get up at four thirty every morning. It's an age thing. Anyway, we came in and got to work, and we hit on the password. I should say the program hit on the password."

Did she say what I think she said? "So you're in?"

"We're in. What should we do?"

"Call Sam and tell him to get down there. I'll be there in forty-five minutes."

"What should we do until then?"

"Break open the babka; I'll bring the coffee. This calls for a celebration."

I tell Laurie what has happened. She tells me that she and Ricky will walk the dogs, and that I should get right down to the office.

When I arrive, Sam is already there, analyzing what they have found. "It's all here. You won't believe how much."

Right now all I'm thinking about is what to do with it. "Can you make a copy of it?"

"Of course. I can have it in less than an hour."

"Good. Do it, and then we tell the cops how to get into the original. I'll get Pete to have their cyber people go over it; I'll tell them what to look for once you tell me what's there."

Sam nods. "That's a plan."

The last three days have moved frustratingly slow.

The police do not move with the cyber speed of Sam Willis; they are properly being painstaking in their analysis and their cataloging of what they are finding.

Richard Wallace and his people are also involved, which I am appreciative of. I think Richard knows where this is heading and understands that the fair thing is to get it there quickly.

He finally calls me. I generally hate talking on the phone, but I've been waiting for this conversation for a while.

"I'm sending you a report on what we've learned," he says. "But it confirms almost everything you thought."

"Excellent. But why did you use the word *almost*?"

"Because it doesn't touch Thomas Roden. It refers vaguely to him, but never by name. There is not enough here to get him. Your boy Darrell is going down for the shootings, but unless he rats out Roden, we can't make that case."

"So where do we stand on Nick's trial?"

"I've got some hoops to jump through on my end, but there is no way we retry this."

"That's not enough, Richard."

"I know. You want a statement declaring him innocent."

"Exactly."

"I believe I can make that happen, especially since Darrell is going down for it. They didn't pull the trigger simultaneously."

"How long will all this take?"

"A day, maybe two."

"Then don't let me keep you . . . go make it happen."

Richard sends me the report on Shaffer's computer, and I gather the whole team to give them an update.

Once I describe all the details, I say, "Sally Montrose and Darrell will never see the light of day again. That takes care of most of the local stuff. The rest has been turned over to the Feds to analyze every one of the malpractice cases and to make the case that they were paid hits. Shaffer's computer information will make that easy. Cynthia Bullock has already been arrested."

"How did these people find Roden and Shaffer?" Corey asks.

"Apparently in various ways, but the majority on the dark web. You can pretty much buy anything there."

"And what happens to Roden?" Corey asks.

"That's the only problem. With what we have, they can't touch him. The investigation is ongoing, but he has insulated himself pretty well."

"Then it's a problem for us," Laurie says.

"How so?"

"Roden has demonstrated that he will remove anything and everyone who has gotten in his way. Wheeler, Shaffer, and the six people at the office. He also tried for Loomis. And you are now at the very top of his list, Andy. The absolute peak."

"I don't see it that way."

"Of course you do. You just don't want to admit it. You destroyed his entire operation. You think he'll just shrug that off?"

"Okay, so I'll be careful for the next couple of weeks. But with all that has happened, Roden will want to stay as far away from this as he can. He'll count himself lucky to have gotten away and let it go."

We leave it there, mainly because there's nothing else we can do with it.

"Let's focus on the positive," I say. "There's plenty of that. I'm hoping Nick will get out tomorrow morning, and then we can have our party tomorrow night."

The meeting breaks up. Everybody leaves except Marcus, who walks over to me.

"Thank you," he says.

"You're welcome."

Then he turns and leaves.

Nick is brought into the meeting room by the guards. He is still handcuffed, which pisses me off.

I haven't kept him informed about the progress we've made the last few days; I didn't want to build his hopes up until we were absolutely sure.

Richard Wallace called me an hour ago, and now we are sure.

"Hey, Andy. What's going on?"

"Actually quite a bit."

He is instantly alert. "What do you mean? Did something happen?"

"First of all, I hope you've got nicer clothes than that." I point to his prison outfit.

"What about my clothes?"

"Well, if you're going to a party tonight, you can't wear that."

"Andy, tell me what you're talking about."

"You're going home." I break into a wide smile. "The charges against you have been dropped; they're going to make an announcement fully clearing you."

"Tell me you're serious."

"I'm serious."

"Now tell me how it happened."

"I will . . . tonight at the party. Right now I have to make sure all the paperwork is done so that we don't have the party without you. You're the guest of honor."

I leave and spend the next three hours cutting through the bureaucracy, which is why Nick is here in the upstairs room at Charlie's for our party. Also here, besides Laurie and me, are Corey and his girlfriend, Dani; Willie and Sondra Miller; Sam Willis; and Hilda and Eli Mandelbaum.

Not here for some reason is Marcus Clark. I would be worried about him if he weren't Marcus Clark. My best guess is he was uncomfortable with the profuse thank-yous that would be coming his way from Nick, so Marcus chose to avoid it.

Nick asks about Daisy, the golden retriever he fell in love with, and I have to disappoint him by saying that she was adopted already. "I'm sorry, but the leg healed and it wasn't fair to make her wait for a home. And there was no guarantee when or if you were getting out."

"I understand. It was a good home, right?"

Willie overhears the conversation and interjects that, yes, it is an excellent home.

I spend some time answering Nick's questions about the case. He keeps asking more; it makes sense that he is anxious to know exactly what nearly ruined his life. His main question is why the killings took place at all.

"Brisker was the target," I say. "He knew something was wrong and he was figuring out what it was. He had his friend there, an insurance executive, to discuss how to deal with it. So they silenced Brisker and killed the others to cover the fact that it was him they were after. They tried to kill Loomis later on for the same reason."

"So they never planned to kill Monty?"

"No, and she had Laura Schauble in the room next door so

that Laura could be a witness to the killer knowing the nickname, and wearing the sneakers, and having the same tattoo."

Nick shakes his hand in amazement. "They really had me nailed. If not for you . . ."

Just then, Nick's friend Rafe shows up late. He's brought a date with him . . .

Daisy.

Daisy sees Nick and runs to him, demonstrating that her leg is just fine, thank you. He starts half laughing and half crying, especially when Daisy immediately flops down on her back so Nick can scratch her stomach.

"I told you she loves this," he says.

"And I told you she got a great home," Willie says. "Yours."

read the story on the internet this morning. It is a small item on the CNN website.

Thomas Roden, a man said to have organized crime connections, jumped or was thrown off the fifth floor of a parking garage in Chicago to his death last night.

The clear implication is that he was murdered, as he did not even have a car in the garage at the time. It is thought to have been a mob-ordered murder.

I think I'm starting to understand Marcus Clark.

ABOUT THE AUTHOR

Brandy Allen

David Rosenfelt is the Edgar Award–nominated and Shamus Award–winning author of almost thirty Andy Carpenter novels, most recently *Dog Day Afternoon*; nine stand-alone thrillers; two nonfiction titles; and four K Team novels, a series featuring some of the characters from the Andy Carpenter series. After years of living in California, he and his wife moved to Maine with twenty-five of the four thousand dogs they have rescued.